MW00415977

Wild Blood
Cyborg Shifters: Book One

***

By Naomi Lucas

Table of Contents

Chapter One:

• • • •

"Katalina, your life is worth more than this."

She frowned, looking at her late grandmother's house. Emotion festered in the pit of her stomach, heavy and hard.

It manifested in her eyes as the blank stare of someone who was looking but not actually seeing. Not focusing. Kat felt the lump grow and expand until it caused her throat to close, making it hard to swallow or hold back the tears that sprang to her eyes.

I'm alone now.

She stood there looking at the rusty old structure with love, fear, and a little bit of uncertainty. The house and everything in it were hers now. Except it wasn't, at least not anymore. She had sold it to the first bidder.

To Kat, it would always remain the possession of the dead woman she had taken care of for the past several years. The last member of her family who she loved had been reduced to a fond memory; a ghost that now took the form of a stone in her gut and the invisible hands encircled her neck.

Kat clicked the button on her key-chip, nearly breaking the small device with the pressure from her thumb. The house shut down. The metal shutters folded over the windows, barred and blacked out, and the alarm system activated.

She hugged herself as her ears twitched. The humming sound of moving metal, a sturdy zip of electricity; the groan of rusted edges filled her ears.

Goodbye, Grandma. I love you more than anything. My life will never be like yours, but I will make it count for something.

She pocketed the key-chip and picked up the single suitcase by her side.

The old house had been sold and today was the last day before the new residents moved in.

The now useless key-chip in her hand would be her only memento. Kat ran her finger over the bump it made in her pocket, before rubbing the back of her hand across her cheeks and clearing her face.

She heard the rumble of a land-flyer settling on the house's landing pad. Her relatives. Kat turned away from the memories with a rushed goodbye and jumped into her own flyer, throwing her bag in the back. The door closed just as her uncle called out. Without looking up, she programmed in her destination as he pounded on the window next to her face.

"Katalina! Get out of the craft."

"Sorry, can't hear you," she mumbled under her breath.

"You can't do this!"

"Watch me."

Her flyer shot into the air just as her uncle started screaming obscenities, only to be drowned out by the rushing wind. With her destination locked in and autopilot enabled, Katalina, for the first time she could remember, felt the heady rush of adrenaline sweep through her.

She leaned her head back against the seat and let the energy of it take over, getting lost in the mire of her thoughts and the strum of her racing heart.

She was headed for the largest interstellar port in New America with no goal in mind; Kat had no plans for the future beyond getting away from the stink of slow, moldering death and her extended family.

They had descended like vultures in the weeks before her grandmother's death. At first, she had been delighted that they were there, that they had wanted to help out; but when the will was read and everything was left to her, things changed.

Earth was no longer her home. She needed to get off its surface before she was suffocated by her own grief.

Whiplash and heartbreak.

Kat wasn't naive about the seven deadly sins, nor was she unfamiliar with greed, but she had hoped she wasn't related to anyone who would succumb to them.

Now that the estate was sold, she was finally taking her grandmother's advice.

"You'll leave this place, even if I have to force you to do it."

The scenery sped by. The old world slowly vanished until high risers and metal structures surrounded her. Kat looked at her bag and took a deep breath. The city opened up like a cracked egg: the guts were a giant space field, miles upon miles of heavily guarded flat ground, all of it surrounded by the metal barriers of commerce.

Huge ships came into view, bigger than she remembered. The battleships and mining freighters couldn't land here. Their girth was so massive, so giant, that it would disrupt Earth's shields and crush the ground. Kat had seen pictures of them–she knew that people could spend their entire lives living on one of those monsters.

They bruised the sky with their thruster output. Once spaceflight had taken off, the weather patterns had never been the same: the massive engines plowed right through the clouds, dispersing them.

Her flyer came to a stop at the intake gate. Her breath quickened and palms dampened with excitement. She allowed her vehicle to be scanned and added to the docking base for storage. It drove her to its new semi-permanent parking spot.

Kat grabbed her bag and hefted it onto her lap before opening her door to the arid heat of the desert city; her lungs filled up with hot, dry air as she tried to get her bearings. With a final glance, she locked up her flyer and headed for the concourse.

Her uncertainty grew with every step.

Kat switched her bag from shoulder to shoulder, trying to alleviate the strain it put on her neck and back.

I have no idea what I'm doing. Her jaw tensed. The entryway loomed before her, beautifully decorated reinforced glass and silver metal; it glistened to the point that it hurt her eyes.

Welcome to space, it said. *Welcome to the gate of hell,* it meant. *Did you know that your survival rate drastically decreases once you leave Earth?* it implied. *Let's explore!*

It said a lot more than that.

With a sigh, Kat walked through the doors. She was greeted by screens and holograms, all projecting and trying to sell her on a new adventure. A commercial cruise around Jupiter. A trip to see the battle monuments on Gliese. She flinched and looked to the next thing: a billboard listing hundreds of jobs.

She walked past it and toward the large, domed windows where stores were set up to overlook the space field. They were up on a plateau, and the view outside showed everything.

Kat lugged her bag to a bench that overlooked the commercial and private vessels; from here, she could watch them enter the atmosphere and shoot up into the stars.

I'll be on one of them before long.

She sat there for some time. People walked by behind her, and her eyes trailed them in the window's reflection. Loved ones coming together, people breaking apart. Kat rubbed her wrists, missing her grandma.

She debated contacting her uncle and going back to her extended family. To stay on Earth and deal with them, curling up in their familiarity.

Kat was pulled out of her thoughts when a woman sat down on the bench next to her.

"You've been here for quite a while. Are you waiting for someone?" she asked. Kat looked at her warily. The woman was older, with greying hair, and draped in scarves.

"Uh, no. No, I'm not waiting for anyone," Kat answered.

"Ah, I supposed that might be the case. We get your kind here every now and then, waiting for something to hit you over the head and change your life. Mmm hmm."

Kat squirmed in her seat. "Didn't realize I had a 'kind.' I wish I'd known about my people before this."

The older woman laughed, hoarse and mirthful. "I once saw a young man sit in this very seat, every day, for days on end, waiting and watching the ships. I went up to him after the third day–my curiosity always gets the best of me–and asked him what he was up to."

"What *was* he up to?" Kat asked, intrigued.

"Well, he was discharged from the military for having a bum leg. He didn't know what to do with the rest of his life, as his whole family was military. He felt hurt, lost, insecure. So after hearing this, I offered him a job."

"Did he take it?"

"He sure did. He's manning my exotic teas booth behind us. Been with me for damned near ten years! Can't get rid of the sucker. He's a good worker, though he doesn't talk enough for my liking so I have to talk for the both of us." The woman rambled on.

Kat looked behind her at the tea booth and saw a middle-aged man pouring a cup for a customer.

The woman continued, "I was the one that hit him over the head that day and made a decision for him. He's great at lifting the heavy stuff. As you may have noticed, this port is large, but only one terminal is still in operation. Everywhere else is barred off and unused, but my tea shop still stands and endures. There's something about a nice cup of tea from another planet, or maybe it's the last chance to drink something from home–"

Kat cut her off, "Why is only one terminal in use?" She eyed the giant ships resting in the distance.

"Oh, honey, you know the answer to that. There's just not enough people anymore. Even for the biggest spaceport in New America. This place should be a bustling bazaar but nope, can't sustain it anymore. What's your name, dear?" The woman was a word racehorse. Kat could understand why the man she hired never talked.

"Katalina. Kat for short."

"What a pretty name! Do you want a job, Kat? You see, my knees are gettin' achy and the long hours, well, are too long these days. John, my employee, is a friendly guy to work with and could use the extra help too. It's hard to find help these days, and who knows? Maybe you and John might like to take over someday. He's a nice man, could use a nice girl. The job comes with free tea."

Free tea, eh?

The port rumbled. Kat turned to see a jet black ship descend from the sky and watched the giant vehicles that drove out to meet it. It looked like a bullet with spindly legs... like a spider. A terrible, black widow of a spider.

"Oh, monster-man is back! Have you ever seen a Trentian in real life, dearie?"

Monster man? Trentian? Kat glanced at the scarved woman. "What? No..."

"We get them here sometimes, they walk by my shop. Once, a diplomat stopped and ordered a drink. Scared me he did. Ordered chamomile of all things.

13

Handsome bugger, though. John was on break that day, and the Trentian asked if I'd join him. You know, out there." She pointed to the sky. "Thought I could be his bride, he did. Me? An old woman on the arm of someone like him? Shooed him off and told him I'm married to my teas. John doesn't believe me. I wonder if monster-man brought us any monsters today?"

Kat turned back toward the ship. It landed with power, a visible plume of smoke and dust shooting away from it as it settled onto the ground. There was a sudden stillness, a sudden silence and her eyes were stuck to it. Nothing could pull her away from the spider.

It looked like a bug. *I hate bugs.* Her hands twitched.

Other people came forward to watch. The shopkeeper next to her turned to someone who appeared at her side.

"Think we'll see another El'Mook? I love their ears."

The back of the ship, or what she thought was the back, opened and the huge vehicles lined up for it. A group of armed men closed in. It was below her and in the distance, but she could still see everything.

A man walked out. Decked out in black, black and unsettling like his ship. They matched.

"Who is he?" Kat asked absently.

"Monster-man? A Cyborg. Scary guy, he works for the government, capturing and containing creatures and plants from all over the known galaxies. He's well-known here. Oh, what do you think that is?"

A huge cage was unloaded, glass and metal barricades enclosed whatever was inside. The Cyborg-monster-man was overseeing the process. Dozens of guns were pointed at the beast. The cage shook with a violent impact from a creature nobody could see.

Whatever it is, it really wants to get out.

Someone murmured, "Nothing I've ever seen before. Don't know how he captures beasts four times his size."

Kat couldn't take her eyes off the man. A black dot in the distance. She was curious about the creature, but the Cyborg commanded her attention and she gave it to him gladly–she just wished that she was closer so she could see him more clearly.

A tingle rushed through her. Her hands clenched at her side. More cages were taken off and loaded into the trucks. Giant plants. Glass tubes filled with strange liquids. Even a cat-like creature with a tail that stretched out for yards was led out by a leash.

It was all over too quickly. The Cyborg and those who had met him walked toward the port and out of her sight.

Kat picked up her bag when a hand rested on her arm. She turned back to the old woman.

"Dearie, the job is yours if you find your way back here. Could always use a pretty face behind the counter. I'd sell more tea with you pouring it." And then the woman was gone.

Kat stood up and looked at the tea stand. Her soul leaned toward the comfortable prospect of an adventure being a tea seller, meeting humans from all over the universe, people traveling to exotic places, all while surrounded by good drinks. The thought of going to sleep at night with a cup of tea next to her.

A heavy thud and a gasp stopped her from choosing that future.

"It's a Cyborg." A tourist stepped back, alarmed.

Kat saw the pathway open up as everyone, not many, backed away.

A man in a grey suit walked beside the large, imposing Cyborg: the monster-man from the spider ship. A woman trailed behind, writing notes. The Cyborg looked like a man, only larger, taller, and perfect, with a face that could've been carved from stone. It was angular...sharp.

So very sharp. He looks angry.

It made it all the more frightening with his thick, arching eyebrows and midnight hair, not quite black, almost a deep, dark blue. It was slicked away from his face to fall down his back, held together by a loose string.

He was white. Not like human white but white as snow, white as a wraith, and the Cyborg almost glowed against the dark clothing he wore.

Monster-man looks like a killer.

"You need another body on board. You can't keep going out there alone."

"I won't be responsible for someone else. I have enough to take care of as is."

Their voices echoed throughout, demanding everyone in the terminal to eavesdrop and witness. Kat forgot all about the tea stand.

"Which is exactly why you need someone to manage you. You won't be responsible for anyone, *they'll* be responsible for *you*. A liaison of sorts. We can't have another incident like last time. If you don't pick an auditor, an assistant, a contact for us, we will pick one *for* you. Resumes have been uploaded onto your console."

"I'm leaving immediately. There's no time to hire a useless–"

"We will pick one for you or we will dissolve your contract and Stryker's and force you to work together." The suit repeated. "Or you can be let go."

They walked past her. She stared wide-eyed at the Cyborg man. Kat was like everyone else in the port.

He glanced at her and she felt the breath get sucked out of her lungs. Then he looked away. The group moved out of earshot. They were gone as quickly as they had arrived.

His eyes. They sizzled her flesh with just a glance.

Kat was dumbstruck. She headed toward the ticketing station and made her way through the gates.

• • • •

Chapter Two

Dommik oversaw his beasts being taken off his ship. To him, they were his lifeblood, his mission. His duty to the people that created him. They each had a story.

The Urgoke from Gliese resembled the ancient Triceratops, the Ewayen from Elyria could have been a mad scientist's dream of flying fish that smelled like citrus, and the Shunkun plants from Tau-Ceti were as smart as chimps and had a taste for fresh meat. He captured them by order, by plea, or just by plain curiosity to be studied by the Earthian Planetary Exploration Division's scientists.

He was waiting for his employers to safely contain his creatures, lest he needed to hunt them across the metropolis. It wouldn't be the first time.

Dommik's fingers tapped the worn black leather stretched over his knee. He wanted to get back to his ship before the EPED found him an assistant.

A goddamned spy. His eyes narrowed as the time ticked by. The grey suit and his young assistant were busy corresponding with the transporters. No one talked to him unless they had to.

He preferred the quiet. It made him a better predator.

Dommik eyed his patrons. *It would take me three shots to down four of them.* But they weren't warriors like him. Just normal people going about their normal jobs, trying to make it through another normal day.

They overlooked the reinforced facility, up high behind thick glass. His creatures were now being handled by xenobiologists and botanists. His fingers stilled on his leg.

"We're having you take the Molucs back. They began to breed, and the scientists chose to tag them and want them released back into the wild. The weather here isn't cold enough to sustain them without them going into heat," the grey suit turned to him just as the truck arrived. Dommik could smell the furry animals from where he sat.

"I told you that before I delivered them."

"The division needed to check them out–"

"Because they breed like rabbits?"

"Because poachers were stealing them off the planet and now they've been found on several other worlds."

He watched as the Molucs passed through quarantine and moved out to board his vessel. They looked like baby dragons, if dragons existed, down to a fuzzy set of wings and a long tail that curled up into a cotton-like ball. He found the peaceful creatures endearing even if they had a tendency to infest.

Dommik stood up, the worn leather of his armor pulled comfortably taut around his large frame.

"Everything looks fine here. I'll make sure the Molucs are checked out by my androids and boarded." He turned toward the exit. His fists clenched at his sides.

"Dommik," the suit called after him, stopping him in his tracks. "You won't be cleared for takeoff until we have a live body on that ship of yours. The EPED can't afford to break protocol for you anymore without eyes on the inside. If you get attacked again..."

Dommik felt the hard edges of his knives hidden under his armor. He felt the leather restrict his palms as his hands released. He heard the man behind him but wouldn't acknowledge the suit's comment. It could hurt a man's pride. A lesser man's pride.

How could an opponent who was significantly weaker than you do anything but try? He felt a small smile twitch at the corner of his lips. It was a hard smile to keep hidden.

There was a reason he liked being out in the wilds alone.

"I get attacked every day. If you don't need me anymore to bring in the beasts then, by all means, send down a spy. I'm sure you could find someone to replace me," Dommik warned.

His fist hit the button at the door and he strode out of the room. He didn't make it three feet when the clatter of heels sounded behind him. He sighed and kept walking.

Mia.

"Dommik, wait, please. It's not what you think." A slender hand clutched his forearm. The man's assistant rattled to a long, awkward stride next to him. His arm was her crutch. "We're not trying to spy on you."

He looked down at the cleaned up and tight blonde. He towered over her slight, put-together frame that wore a pencil skirt and white blouse as accessories. Eyelashes thick with black mascara and cherry red lips parted as she met his eyes.

"I work alone."

"You don't have to be alone. Hire me. I'll stay out of your way, I'll stay quiet. I'm sure we could come to a mutual agreement."

"I work alone, Mia," he repeated. "I don't have time to babysit." Her bust strained against her shirt as she inhaled. Dommik looked away and kept walking.

"Don't be like that, Cyborg. I'm the best bet you have. I know the job, I know the people, and I know you," Mia continued. Her argument was sound, but the idea of having her smell up his ship with heavy perfume hurt any chance she might have had. He imagined how it would stick to him as he went out on hunts. The smell would give him away.

Beasts from nearby planets would know of his presence.

"You don't *know* me, Mia, and you're not getting on my ship." He peeled her fingers off his arm. "I'm not your free ticket to see the universe or a way to sleep yourself into a better position. All you would be is bait up there. You're pretty enough–find someone else to throw yourself at."

"Fuck you, Dommik, I actually liked you. I would have been good by your side. Good luck with whoever they send you. You sure as hell will regret it." She stopped following him.

"I'll make sure to send you a missive when I do."

"Dommik, wait!" Mia called after him, her tone changed. He sighed and turned around.

"What?"

"Please be safe out there." She waved her hand at him and without a second glance, walked back toward the quarantine facility.

Dommik could only think of her rancid perfume as she vanished around a corner. Mia may have been his best bet as a co-worker, but he had an even better bet in mind: no one.

He passed back through the gates that led to the last working terminal at the port. If he made it fast enough, if he left without being fully restocked, he may escape with the Molucs without another creature in tow.

Another human who would stare at him like an oddity. The denizens of the port stopped and gaped at him, moving out of his path and whispering behind cupped hands.

He wasn't just a Cyborg in their eyes. He was a miscreation. Dommik knew all the names that people called him behind his back. It was easy to hear whispers, even those from across a room, with the technology built into his ears. His work required the best in perception enhancements and he took it seriously.

The money that he didn't funnel back into the ship went straight into his head as newer waves of cybernetic enhancements rolled out. Scope sight, hearing, a keen sense of smell. It made him the hunter he was today.

He wouldn't call himself the best. There were other Cyborgs that hunted, other Cyborgs he would even call *friends* that did what he did. Sometimes he was called in on a special project or asked to help another hunt. Sometimes teamwork was a necessary evil. One he took better than other Cyborgs.

Dommik wasn't afraid of cutting the throat of a corrupt politician. Or even taking a side job every once in a while to take out a person he thought deserved it.

Even humans were monsters. They just hid it behind a suit of flesh and honeyed words. He owned up to his crap.

The sticky smell of human musk, potent lotion, and processed food made him hurry his steps. Even as his tech reconfigured for the increased speed, silence was always on his mind. Dommik left the semi-busy terminal behind, seeing his gate at the end of the hall.

He saw a girl sitting on a drab suitcase next to his exit to the field.

How? It's been three minutes since I turned down Mia.

As Dommik got closer he recognized the female from earlier. The brief eye contact they had made as she became one of the many gaping bystanders. She didn't breathe when she looked at him. He hadn't understood why. The girl was quiet.

She tapped her cheeks and sighed. *She isn't quiet now.*

Dommik stood over her. His shadow blocked out the light. Her delayed reflexes annoyed him.

Death comes so easy to the weak.

The girl looked away from her hands and slowly up at him. Green eyes met his, wide and startled. He walked past her to his gate.

The picture of her solidified in his mind. Short copper curly hair that framed rounded cheeks with a splattering of freckles. Her hair was pushed back behind her ears, but small tendrils rebelled and fell forward. If he ever had a missive to hunt down and kill a sprite, he knew what to look for, who to look for.

"I'm here for the job," she said.

"There is no job." Dommik opened the door and walked through. A thump sounded behind him, a gasp and a bang. The girl forced her way through the doors and followed him. He repeated without turning, "It's already been filled."

She huffed, keeping pace. "I don't see anyone else here."

They walked out into the open airfield. Dommik took a deep breath of almost fresh air, filled with the smell of dust and engine exhaust. And the subtle smell of the girl behind him that he couldn't place.

"I don't need you and if you keep following me, you'll have security on you within seconds. You're not authorized to be out here."

"You haven't even given me a minute. Look," she breathed heavily, stumbling behind him, "I heard what you do. You're not a monster!"

Dommik stopped.

He turned around.

His ship loomed over them like a wave about to crash.

She continued with a gulp, "I heard what the others were saying. You're not a monster." Emerald green eyes met his again.

"And you're an idiot."

The girl dropped her bag and crossed her arms. "I'm not."

"I'm a Cyborg. I hunt for *fun*. I kill for *fun*. I am the fiend everyone says I am. If you're looking for an adventure," she flinched at the word, "or trying to prove something, find someone else. If you're looking for a Cyborg to fuck, join the breeding facility. You'll be dead within a week of working for me." Dommik turned toward his ship's hatch and watched as the Molucs were led into his high-tech menagerie. "I told the EPED, I work alone."

"So you don't have an assistant." Her eyes narrowed at him.

Dommik warned, "Dead within a week."

"That would be my problem, not yours."

He tensed as she followed him into his ship, breathing heavily and pulling her bag behind her. It screeched over the concrete. He moved toward his androids who were settling the Molucs into their temporary home. He heard the girl gasp as long, white fuzzy wings extended out behind their bulletproof habitat. His robots programmed the interior to mimic the Moluc's planet's icy ecosystem.

Their fuzzy fur extended out, threatening, like a spooked cat. The pair of dragon-like creatures hopped around the home they knew from many moons before. He couldn't be sure if they were upset for being moved again or reluctant to be back on familiar ground.

The girl moved up to the glass as the creatures buried themselves into the quickly accumulating snow until they disappeared under the drifts.

"Get off my ship," he growled. Seeing the girl, so unlikely and wrong on his ship, and in his space unnerved him. He had half a mind to throw her into a cell like one of the other countless animals he transported.

The girl clutched her bag, her hand clenched on the handle of the suitcase as he stepped forward and invaded her personal space. She was tall but still a head shorter than him. He could hear her heart race, could sense the tension wrack her body, could even smell the desperation and courage come from her.

They stood there, staring at each other, neither one backing down and slowly, strangely, something shifted between them. It was muted and weak, but it was there.

Her soft, round face gave her the appearance of a pixie. The tiny curling tendrils of her hair stood to attention and didn't move as they should have. It was a disservice to her features. They were meant to move in a breeze.

I've never had a fairy before. Dommik broke the moment and looked around at all of his empty cages.

"Let me explain," she said, pulling his eyes back to her. She set the bag down. Bright green eyes stabbed him. A soft stab, but a stab nevertheless. "I need this job."

Dommik hardened. "There is no job." He grabbed the back of her shirt, tore the bag out of her hand, and threw them both off his ship.

Chapter Three:

• • • •

Kat stumbled out onto the airfield in shock. She glanced back at the Cyborg, but he had already turned around and disappeared into his ship. The strange off-world animals in the snow-filled glass cube shuffled and hopped around. Three androids moved throughout, preparing the strange menagerie, importing and exporting materials.

She was determined to be hired as his assistant. Something in her gut, in her boring lifelong existence as a middle-class land-dweller, wanted to be on the spider-ship. She was curious about the Cyborg, the monster-man, and why fate would taunt her with overhearing this job opening, on this day, at that moment, where she had been standing?

Kat was a home-nurse, a hospice care provider before her grandmother got sick. She had been around death her entire life, first with her parents, then with her patients, only to end up closing the eyes of her nana.

Her parents had died from the same illness.

The one she was afraid of flowing through her very veins as she stood there gawking.

She knew what this man did for a living. If she could be on his ship, be a part of the research of the specimens he provided, she might just find a way to save herself, though she could not save her family. Why else would the opportunity present itself?

Why else would I be here?

Kat picked up her bag and walked back up the ramp. *I'm doing this.* The Cyborg was nowhere in sight.

One of the androids stopped what it was doing and approached her.

"Please state your business."

"I'm the new hire."

The robot cocked its head while its face flickered. "There is no new hire. There are only resumes. Please state your business."

Kat dropped her bag and opened it, pulling out her console. She projected the screen and pulled up her resume. "Here is my resume." The android pulled it from her projection and into its own system. "I was just hired. I might not be in your system yet."

"Very well, Katalina Jones. Your file has been added to the list. Our master has not authorized additional personnel, but we are not cleared for takeoff until we have a new unit. It is possible."

The android appeared to be thinking.

She had never dealt with an android before, not of this caliber at least. In the medical field, she had seen many operate and work med-slats and cryo-pods from a distance. She had been a lowly care provider with a certification to run the instruments and provide psychological relief. It had allowed her to take care of the sick at homes and hospices but no more. Some people still preferred a human over a machine.

"I was hired by voice contract, minutes ago," she lied, watching the bot. "Why else would I have clearance to be on the airfield or on this spacecraft? Or why have my luggage next to me?"

The android blinked with a series of numbers.

Kat rubbed the tiny key-chip in her pocket. She looked at the other two androids that were ignoring them.

"The ship is readying for takeoff. The probability is higher." The machine stood there unmoving, undeciding.

A voice called out behind her, the man and the woman from before were at the end of the ramp. "Who are you?" the blonde with the tablet called out.

"The new hire," Kat answered, beginning to sweat. *Oh shit. I'm going to get arrested.*

Her bag was yanked out of her hand for the second time that afternoon. The android walked further into the ship with her belongings. "Come this way, Katalina Jones. Takeoff is commencing."

"He hired you!?" the blonde guffawed. Kat looked at her and then back at the android. The ship came to life with a buzz.

"He picked my resume out of the list," she turned to the humans and answered. The man narrowed his eyes.

He spoke up, "You're not an EPED employee. Your resume isn't on that list. Who are you?"

The gate began to close.

"What the fuck, Mason? I'm supposed to be his assistant."

"We'll get to the bottom of this."

The gate slowly made the sky disappear as it fell from the top of the ship. Kat had seconds to decide. Seconds.

Sweat soaked her shirt as she realized what she had done, as she watched the hatch tick away her choice, solidifying her actions. *Find a cure. Go on an adventure. Get arrested. Deal with a monster of a man.* One thought stood out amongst the rest. *I've never left Earth before.* The importance of her thoughts did not come in any order. Kat could hear the robots shuffle behind her.

The man yelled out, "You'll be tried as a stowaway, a spy! If your resume isn't on that list, you'll never fly again!"

"Katalina Jones, you must follow me."

She watched as the two people yelled and argued, only for a moment in time as the slit grew smaller. Her heart raced as she glanced at the glass overlook of the port.

No tea.

"I'm on the list!" Kat yelled at the last second. *Goodbye, chamomile.*

Her fate sealed shut.

The ship hummed to life as the android with her bag led her out of the giant facility and into the tunnels of her new home.

After several turns through dark metal corridors, lights burned low to resemble an old, gloomy warehouse. The robot stopped at a door. A door amongst doors. Kat's hand slapped the wall as the ship quaked under her feet.

The inconspicuous door slid open to reveal a room. So small it only fit a single cot, lifted high off the ground so a desk-like slat sat beneath it. There was an uncomfortable looking metal stool anchored to the wall. The other side was a blank steel-grey wall with several hooks lined across it and a small, circular fixture was on the low ceiling that cast a bright white, penetrating light across the space.

The android placed her bag on the metal slat.

"These are your quarters, Katalina Jones."

"Call me Kat," she mumbled, stepping into her new home.

"Registered." The door zipped closed behind her, the android gone. She turned back toward it, but it didn't reopen. Her fingers slipped across the lukewarm panel and plastic material.

A quick gut-wrenching shock of queasiness punched her in the stomach. She, all at once, felt heavy and lightweight. Kat moved away from the door and grabbed the bars of the desk, not knowing what to expect during takeoff. She held on as if her life depended on it, her palms slick with sweat and her eyes wrenched closed.

It was over quickly. At least she thought so, never having experienced leaving the atmosphere, unable to see what's happening outside her room. She only assumed.

All she knew was that she had made it onto the Cyborg's ship. That she now had a job and that she didn't know how to get out of her room.

Kat lifted herself to her feet and opened her bag, taking out her network device once again. She sat on the ground where her hand still held onto the bar and opened her console.

Network error.

I don't have access? It was unheard of on Earth.

Kat tried to link to the ship but was denied. The lights flickered above. She glanced back at the door, got to her feet, and kicked her bag under the desk.

She stepped up onto a ladder that led to her bed. It had no coverings or no mattress. Her hand slid across the rails.

She made a mental checklist as her eyes drifted across the room.

I need bedding. I need network access. I need a way to tell time. But first... Her eyes landed on the shut panel. *I need to figure out how to open the door.*

••••

DOMMIK STEERED HIS ship out of Earth's commercial airways, overriding the planetary defense system to allow himself off the world. The EPED had nullified his shield access until their demands were met. But it really couldn't stop him, nor could it stop others from entering. It just marked the disturbance. Regardless, the defense satellites would trail him.

If he was a threat, they would shoot him down. He could feel the link of dozens of them coming to life.

He ignored the hails as the reps from the EPED tried to contact him. Mia and her insipid begging came to mind.

His help with procuring the wild plants and animals from across the universe was contingent on one thing: he worked alone. He worked alone and unhindered. That was why he had a staff of androids on his ship.

Dommik peeled off his black vest and straps–the tiny weapons hidden within–all while kicking off his boots until he was wearing nothing but his worn leather pants.

The chilly, nearly scentless air of his ship breezed past his muscles and filled his nose, cleansing the pungent rot of industry and sweat still there.

He fixated on one scent in particular. The unidentifiable smell of the pixie that had hounded him just an hour before. The smell could only be described as something new, something fresh, like many of the scents on the barely habitable planets he visited. He bunched his muscles, feeling the strain of his warped body tighten around him.

His mind wandered to the wild tendrils around her cute face and the piercing green eyes that matched his threatening stare. The dusting of freckles across her pale features. He hardened as he pictured his very own fairy trapped behind a glass cage.

Dommik looked down at his skin, almost perfect and so very much human. But beneath the outer layer was something wrong and monstrous. He grabbed his cock through his pants and yanked it, annoyed with the ever-insistent need to mate.

Because he was a fiend.

And it had nothing to do with him being a Cyborg. He was one of a handful of later edition Cyborgs that could shift. That had dozens of animalistic instincts from countless places and times coded into them. The shifter Cyborgs were different from his fellow brethren. Normal Cyborgs couldn't shift; they always retained their humanoid shape.

The shifters remained in close contact with each other, designed with a pack mentality, but still kept each other at arm's length.

Even now, as he watched the stars zip past, his ship on autopilot to the winter-world of the Molucs, he wanted to darken the mechanical lights of his bridge until he was covered in a blanket of darkness. Where he was the most *alive.*

33

His heavy hand still gripped his shaft between his legs, his fingers applying pressure, squeezing it through the thick material, but his cock had a mind of its own. The thick mushroom head of it squeezed through the buckles at his pelvis.

A tiny bead of precum wetted the tip of his bulge. His animal instincts began to take over. His humanity faded away as he pictured the copper-haired girl stripped naked and waiting for him in his menagerie, panting and doe-eyed in her cage. She couldn't speak, couldn't function, moaning in heat and waiting for him to mount her hard from behind.

His little sprite, losing the ability to fly as he held her trapped under his body, pinned to the floor with his cock.

Dommik squeezed the head of his shaft, refusing to free it, losing himself in the fantasy. A terrible need to subdue came over him. His little fairy with the long legs cried helplessly for release.

His little fairy that was stripped of her wings.

The door swished open behind him. Dommik grunted and squeezed his crotch, mentally saying farewell to the girl in his mind, leaving her unfulfilled and breathless.

Bin-Two stepped into his stark bridge. He swiveled his seat and faced the robot.

"Dommik-One, the creatures in the lab have settled into their habitats. Molucs 1-8456 and 1-8457 melted the snow particles during takeoff but have since fallen asleep with tranquilizers distributed by Bin-One. We have received numerous acquisitions from the Earthian Planetary Exploration Division. What is your request?" Bin-Two stood erect and uncaring that Dommik had his dick half out of his pants.

He leaned forward and rested his elbows on his knees.

"Keep the Molucs fed and euphoric. We're headed for their homeworld before we stop off at Ghost City. Access has been granted to you with the current coordinates. Ignore the Exploration Division, I'll take care of them." Dommik turned back toward his console to deal with the hails and defense satellites. He opened up his most insistent communication. Mia appeared flustered and angry on the screen. Anger looked good on her.

"Accepted. What should Bin-One do about the new hire?" Bin-Two asked.

Dommik stopped. Mia opened her mouth. He had opened a communication too soon.

"What the hell, Cyborg? You take a nobody over me!? She's not even an EPED employee." Mia's sing-song voice raged through the channel. He didn't hear it. "Why don't you have a shirt on?"

He swiveled his seat to face the android. "What did you say?" His still-hard cock twitched.

"Dommik! Face me, dammit–" Mia's voice disappeared as he cut their connection off.

"Accepted. What should Bin-One do about the new hire?" the robot repeated.

"New hire?" he asked slowly.

"Katalina Jones. Resume integrated. Placed in quarters room one. Needs to be integrated. The Earthian Planetary Exploration Division is requesting her credentials and network access for contact, verification, and onboarding."

Dommik got to his feet and stormed out of the bridge, leaving the hails and Bin-Two behind.

He knew he couldn't trust fairies.

Chapter Four:

. . . .

Kat couldn't disassemble the metal furniture in the room, not without tools, and try as she might, she could not pull the stool away from the desk. It was anchored to the floor.

She huffed and crossed her arms over her torso as she eyed her room for the hundredth time. Her stomach growled from hunger. She knew her limitations and with her limited resources–a bag filled with only personal effects–she had no real chance to get out.

Not even to use the lavatory.

A noise sounded outside her door, distant but getting closer. *The android? Footsteps. Heavy footsteps...the Cyborg.*

Kat stiffened and faced the inevitable.

The door slipped open without a sound, and for a moment, she resented it with every fiber of her being.

The Cyborg stood on the other side, quick-fire rage crossed his features. Kat took a step back.

He dominated the doorway, and was big enough to be the door itself. Her pulse quickened as her eyes left his face and trailed down to his half-naked body. Dark pants hugged him, but that was it. Even his feet were bare.

A sliver of fear coursed through her as he took a heavy step into her room. It was too small for the both of them. He stared her down with dark eyes that had a gleam of evil in them.

Kat finally looked at him for what he was, a hunter, a malformation, a predator. Before, he was just a mysterious and intriguing entity; now he was a man who looked like he wanted to strangle her.

Kat swallowed. "You opened the door." He continued to stare at her, the muscles of his arms twitching as if he were trying to restrain himself. She continued, "I need network allowance."

Her face twisted. *I should've asked for his name. Please don't kill me.*

His hand reached out and closed around her throat. Tight, menacing, but gentle. And big. She knew he could crush her but hoped that he wouldn't.

"You shouldn't be here," he growled.

"I'm your new assistant, Katalina. Kat for short," she blustered. The body heat radiating off his chest enveloped her.

"Did you think it was smart? Lying your way into my ship and past my androids? One that is often filled with beasts and dangerous pathogens? There's a reason I work alone. I could kill you, I could do anything to you, and there is no one who could save you."

His hand gradually loosened and fell back, his fist clenched at his side. Kat took a deep breath.

"I needed the job," she said slowly. "I heard what you do–"

"Hunt," he interrupted. "Stalk. Sometimes kill."

"You help colonization efforts and you help find cures."

The rage on the man's face lifted just enough to show a twinge of curiosity in his eyes. She crossed her arms over her chest again, feeling like she needed armor against his gaze.

"Pretty words for what I actually do, what I like to do."

"You still do it, though. I want to help..." Her eyes kept drifting down his body to take in his sculpted chest. Kat wanted to look lower, take the entire Cyborg in, but she didn't.

"You're an idiot. There's no way you can help." He turned to leave.

"I'm a nurse. Wait! I've been around death my whole life. I help people die. I've helped so many people die. I want to be around life for a while, and I want to help people live now. Please." She grabbed his arm. A charge of static electricity zapped her hand. Kat jumped back as the shock coursed through her. She looked at her palm, expecting to see a burn, a blister, or pink skin, but there was nothing.

The Cyborg shuddered as if he was shaking the feel of her off of him. The muscles on his arms flexed and her eyes were drawn to them, her stinging palm forgotten.

"You shouldn't touch me."

"Why? Because you'll shock me?"

"I'm not used to it. I may react badly."

He walked out of the room.

Kat gaped as he disappeared around the corner. His looming presence was missed immediately and for some reason his words made her pity him.

He makes a better door than this stupid metal panel. At least I could get through him if I tried hard

39

enough. And with that thought, she quickly stepped out of her room. The door zipped closed behind her. She looked back at it and then around at the empty, dark passageway of the ship. She had no idea where to go. The Cyborg was gone.

She brushed her tingling palm against her pants and started walking down the direction he had gone.

Why is it so damned dark? The shadows thickened around her, only lifting away every several yards by a dim red light.

Kat called out, "Hello?"

She turned the corner and ran right into him. He wasn't a door this time but a wall. Once again, she found herself jerking back, her heart pounding.

"Follow me," he said roughly.

Kat nodded and stayed on his heels. He led her down a short path until they faced a ladder that went up into a closed hatch. They hadn't walked far.

The Cyborg continued, "This level houses the living areas of the operations crew, and if you turn around and go back the way you entered, you'll find where we keep the specimens. This ladder and everything above is off-limits. If I catch you on one of the upper levels, you'll be thrown in one of the habitats until we reach the next planet. And, Katalina, most of these planets you don't want to be stranded on."

"What's up there?" she asked. He turned to face her. Darkness cloaked his naked chest from her view. The glint of black eyes appeared wider and hollower in the darkness, like the pits of a human skull, the sockets wide and empty.

"The bridge and the living quarters of the main crew."

"So you have a crew?" She scooted to the side as he walked by. She didn't want them to touch again, his warning still clear as day in her head. But the heat that he gave off was an invisible beacon to her within the cold confines of the ship.

"I have androids."

"And me." Kat had to add for good measure. She was met with silence.

He led her back past her room and into an empty lavatory station with multiple shower pods. The Cyborg didn't say anything as he led her through the short, dark hallways, past many doors that she assumed were more living units until they reached the end of their short trek. The area opened up abruptly and she recognized it as the entryway the android from earlier had led her through.

The thick metal slipped silently into the walls as multiple laser shields deactivated. Kat cringed away from the sudden light.

It glowed ruby red before it turned green. Just beyond was another laser barrier and beyond that was the menagerie. She could see the giant glass enclosures through the lights.

When the Cyborg stepped up to the second blockade, it too went green and vanished.

Kat followed him into the giant, multi-level facility. It was as bright as the ship was dark.

Her companion walked further into the cavernous space to an open door. He grunted, "Are you coming?"

She tried to catch a glimpse of the fluffy dragon-like creatures from earlier. One of the androids was next to its enclosure, working at a projected console.

Kat scurried across the space and into the open room. It was filled with computers and holographic screens, wires and buttons, and blinking lights. Some of the screens were turned on to show empty glass cages. Some had creatures on it while others were blacked out.

The Cyborg held out a chair for her. "Sit," he demanded.

She sat.

A blush crept up her neck, over her beating pulse, until it flooded her cheeks. Kat was embarrassed by how easily his commands worked on her, even his unspoken ones. Her hands twitched against her thighs, unsure on what to do, as he leaned over her and typed something onto the screen. The heat of his bare chest made it hard for her to breathe.

I won't look. I won't look. I really want to look. His solid, glorious, white-as-a-spirit chest was directly behind her. His arm was over her shoulder. The Cyborg jailed her between him and the desk. The smell of metal and heat filled her senses as he continued to type, unaffected.

The heat coming off of his body was enough to make her sweat. His long blue-black hair fell over his arm and tickled her cheek.

"You're added to the system." His arms stayed like pillars on either side of her head.

Kat tried to ignore them as she turned to face him. "Thank you." His dark eyes filled her vision and his nostrils flared.

"Are you sniffing me?"

"You smell good." The Cyborg leaned in and smelled her again. Kat veered back, alarmed. His eyes never left hers.

Her stomach growled. He unpinned her and glanced down at her belly before he lifted away. One of his fingers whispered over a wayward curl of her hair, a slight tug, indiscernible but for the trail of goosebumps down her arms.

Kat swallowed. "So what do I do now?"

"You do your job and stay out of my way. You'll respond to the EPED and tell them that I hired you. They may give you hell. You deserve it." He stepped away and the warmth went with him. "I don't like liars, I don't like people in general, but you're here now and so I will use you as I see fit." He turned to leave.

Kat called after him, "What's your name?"

The Cyborg paused, his back once again turned toward her. "Monster," he said eventually. "Since that's what I am."

He left her there, shivering and uncertain at the computer, confused about the tense exchanges they shared. She had never dealt with a Cyborg before and wondered if they all acted the same way. Kat lifted her still tingling palm to her nose and sniffed.

I wonder what I smell like.

An android walked in holding a protein bar and a bottle of water. She drew her hand away from her nose as it placed the nourishment on the desk.

"Thank you."

"You're welcome, Katalina Jones."

Kat studied the silver and bronze machine, taking it in, only to look past it at the open door, questioning where the Cyborg had gone off to. It didn't sit well with her.

She looked back at the android. "What is your master's name?"

"Dommik-One. Please eat, Katalina Jones. He demands it."

Hmm...

"Call me Kat. Does he demand a lot?" she asked, opening up the protein bar. She still had to pee, but her need for food outweighed her need to relieve herself.

"We are androids. We're programmed to follow all orders by the Master."

She eyed the machine. "Would you follow my orders?"

"We will follow Katalina Jones's orders only if they do not impede Dommik-One, if they are humanly reasonable based on our programmed standards, and they do not require us to abandon or jeopardize previously assigned tasks," it stated monotonously.

Kat gulped down her water while the android stood beside her. The silver and bronze robot was shaped like a human with two arms and two legs but was otherwise androgynous. It had no other discerning features and it had no face. The machine was just a simulated human with a screen where its eyes and nose should be.

She looked down. It had no sexual organs and in a way, that relieved her. Kat wasn't opposed to sex-bots; she just didn't want them to be the ones who would be her only co-workers.

"Is there a bathroom in here?"

The robot handed her a thin bracelet. "This will allow you access to everywhere our Master has deemed okay." Kat took the circlet and put it on her wrist. "If you don't want to wear it, there are codes you can memorize for each door. Follow me for the lavatory."

Kat twisted the thin metal over her wrist. It was hot, unusually so. The android led her out of the facility and back into the main ship. The dark passages from before engulfed them. They stopped in front of the lav door.

"When you are done, go back to your quarters, the rest cycle is about to begin."

The light of the android's face lit up the space. It made the shadows outside their periphery even darker. *Dark enough for a lurker.*

When she finished up in the cold, wet room, it was gone.

Kat quietly made her way to the open door of her quarters. A trickle of fear ran up her spine. She looked down each end of the hallway, but she couldn't see far beyond the gloom.

"Hello?" she called out. "Dommik?" she whispered under her breath.

Kat shook herself and quickly walked into her room. The door shut behind her and the lights came on. Her fingers trailed through her curls as she took a deep breath and closed her eyes. Her heart raced. And it wasn't entirely with fear. The image of the Cyborg's muscled chest filled her head, his depthless dark eyes that made him ghoulish in the shadows, and his sculpted arms trapping her in the chair.

The blistering heat he radiated.

She heard footsteps outside her panel door, heavy and slow, stopping right on the other side. Kat turned around to face whatever came through.

But they picked up again and faded away.

• • • •

THAT NIGHT, HOURS LATER, Kat's eyes sprang open. She was curled on chemically cleaned bedding that had magically appeared, and a loose cotton blanket that smelled like the Cyborg covered her to the tip of her nose.

The footsteps had returned, but accompanying them was the sound of clicking. Metal on metal.

Once again they stopped outside her room. The lights were set to dim and she twisted her head on her flat pillow to stare at the closed door. She could see him, in her mind, right on the other side of the barrier, standing there breathless like she was.

Kat moved her fingers into the blanket and tucked it tighter under her chin. Her body was flushed despite the cold temperature of the ship.

Her eyes burned. She refused to blink. The footsteps had yet to move.

Part of her wanted Dommik to walk through the door. Part of her wanted him to go away.

Kat licked her lips and waited until time slowed down and sleep gripped her remaining energy and pulled her under into its blissful throes. She fell asleep without ever realizing it had taken her. She never heard the footsteps leave.

. . . .

Chapter Five

"Is the girl strapped in for warp?" Dommik asked the android, Bin-One, at his back.

"Yes, Master, Bin-Three is with her. Would you like a status report?" the robot asked.

"No," he mumbled, even though he did. He hadn't approached his new employee, his assistant, his slave since the first day; that was only because of his irritation.

She had finished the government mandated training to work the job she fought her way into. The girl, Katalina, had begun accumulating data from the creatures on board. She was now sending updates to the EPED, and Mia was her main point of contact.

Dommik's lips twitched at that.

They wanted Katalina to do more, but he refused to allow her clearance to do so. His androids were capable of everything the girl could do...except free-thinking and free-will.

The fresh smell of her clung to him like a parasite. It stayed with him wherever he went. He couldn't sterilize it, he couldn't wash it off, he couldn't get away from it. It made getting through the day unpleasant, and the night agonizing.

So he avoided her. If the girl knew what he really was, what he had done, or what he did currently, she would run screaming. They always did.

It's best to keep her and stay away. If it isn't her, it's Mia... He couldn't even imagine the horror of having Mia spy on him while being stuck with her on his ship. She was desperate to get off of Earth. Dommik couldn't bring himself to feel bad for her. Mia was good at her job, but she was stuck soil-side doing it and she didn't make enough cash to travel.

He turned to Bin-One. "Brace, we're cleared for warp." He turned back to his console, well used and faded, and thrust his ship into lightning speed. By the time the colors of the stars and planets flooded his vision, he was a system away from the Molucs' home-world.

The steel wiring and plates in his body shook from the pressure.

His cyber-mechanical makeup was different than that of any normal Cyborg. Everything on his interior was completely fabricated, even his biological organs were fabricated. His brain was human, but it was filled with more circuitry and wiring than nerves and blood vessels.

Dommik thumbed his chest, finding the plates just below his muscles, and wondered when he would have to upgrade them next. He had suffered internal mechanical damage on several occasions, one of those occasions had been recent and was why he had a live body on board now. Those pieces had been replaced.

After he dropped off the Molucs, he had a debt to pay.

The ship settled back into auto-pilot as he put their course toward the snow-covered planet. He ran his hand over his face.

"How did the girl do?" he asked the android as it detached from the wall supports it used.

Dommik knew the girl had never been space-side before. Kat had been green with it as her eyes had taken in everything. She had taken him in in the same way.

Wide emerald orbs with specks of gold. No matter how hard he tried to delete her from his thoughts, she refused to go away. The girl had reacted to him in the way he liked best: fear. Uncertainty. Trepidation. All of them had flashed over her wild features but her voice intoned otherwise.

Stubborn courage.

"Katalina Jones had an adverse reaction to the warp, Master."

He turned to the robot. "How so?"

"She ran to the lavatory. Bin-Three is outside the door right now. Bin-Three hears sickness from her."

Nausea wasn't unusual for a first-timer.

Dommik turned back to the console and double-checked his coordinates. He could see the white ball of the planet in the distance outside the glass. The Molucs would need to be prepped for send-off. *I'll have to encounter Katalina.* His cock jerked at the thought.

It didn't matter that he was a Cyborg: he was still a man in many ways, and the rest of him was bestial, animalistic, and those instincts were kicking in. They became harder to control when he caught a trail of her scent on one of his robots or when he passed her quarters at night.

He wasn't designed to breed with females; he had been designed for theory and for war. A war that

49

lasted nearly a hundred years before it ended with mutual hatred and acceptance. A war to fight for control of the Milky Way galaxy. An endless battle against another alpha species.

The Trentians were intelligent but protective and had odd, mystic ways about them. Where Earthians worshiped knowledge, the Trentians worshiped their god, Xanteaus, and everything the alien god mandated.

But he was different and so were his brothers. *Why not try and add animal DNA into a Cyborg? Let's find out what happens...*

He was created, tested, and approved, and the part of him that was a beast wanted to be unleashed. Dommik flexed his fingers before he unzipped his pants.

No matter how many times he had sterilized his ship, bathed himself, or had the androids go through quarantine procedures, the smell lingered. He still couldn't put a name to her scent, only that it was *hers* and it was wild like her hair. It was fresh and clean and completely erotic to him.

The white planet grew closer. Dommik tapped his fingers, deciding what to do. His blood wanted sex. He wanted the girl with copper curls who had only entered his life days ago.

The blood of beasts. He gripped his dick and squeezed. Thoughts of her flooded his head, legs spread and wet sex. His palm moved up and down his hard length as his blood pooled hard and painful in the cusp of his hand. The tip of his cock pointed high and taut, straining and desperate. His fingers curled around the large head and massaged it as he thrust into his hand.

Freckles and green eyes beneath me. He released himself just long enough to spit into his palm and continue. The heated saliva did nothing but relieve a little pressure and fuel his thoughts. *Curls wrapped around my fingers, damp and slick against my lips.*

He came with a grunt and his cum shot into his hand. It dripped down his wrist and back onto his still-hard cock.

His ship had reached its destination. The white, swirling planet filled his vision and brightened the bridge with its reflection from a nearby star. Everything glowed around him, even his own sperm. Dommik flicked the seed from his hand and located a nearby cleaning cloth, wiping it over him. The smell of his cum lingered in the air and for the hundredth time, he programmed the sanitization units to run.

"Bin-One, I want you to land the ship in the exact coordinates from our last visit. Once we've settled into the snow drifts, release the hatch." He turned to the android, buckling his pants. "Keep the systems secure and the current diagnostics running. Send a signal to Stryker and tell him to meet me at Ghost City."

The android moved to follow his orders as he stepped out of the bridge. He pushed his long hair back and tied it at the base of his neck. Slowly, he regained himself and found the control he needed to proceed. His fingers gripped the hatch that led down to the girl and the menagerie.

Dommik dented the metal wheel.

• • • •

KAT WIPED THE BACK of her hand over her mouth, staring into the receptacle. Her stomach was tied in knots, and she could have sworn her heart had burst. There had been no forewarning of the impending warp. If she had known, she wouldn't have eaten breakfast just prior.

Feeling her senses come back to her, she got up and splashed water over her face and into her mouth. She shook out her curls and headed back to the chamber, feeling queasy but refreshed.

The android, Bin-Three, followed her. He was always within eyesight of her in any of the public areas. The robot kept constant tabs on everything she did and stopped her from doing anything that would upset the '*Master.*' She wasn't naive, and knew the Cyborg was watching her.

He just has his minions do it for him. Kat wasn't sure if she cared that he kept his distance. The dark corridors of the ship were scary enough without having an angry Cyborg creeping around.

But he always visited her at night. Every rest cycle since that first day, she stayed awake until the footsteps sounded outside her door. She hadn't fallen asleep until she heard them leave since her first night.

Kat entered the large laboratory, her eyes adjusting to the lights. The pinging sound of an incoming call rattled from the console room and she sighed audibly. The EPED didn't trust her.

Well... I listened to you, Grandma. I would count this as an adventure even though I'm alone with a bunch of machines, some alien creatures, and a pissed off employer.

It had taken her some time and research to run the reporting system for Mia, and no matter how accurate or how thorough her information was, it was never good enough. The girl disliked her and Kat wasn't quite sure why. The EPED wanted constant coordinate updates, data based on the living organisms onboard, as well as additional information and evaluation from her. So she watched the androids and for the Cyborg as much as they watched her.

No wonder he didn't want to hire anyone.

Mia and her superior wanted more information on Dommik, but she had none to give them. They believed her that he kept his distance, but they didn't believe he stayed away *all the time.*

He comes in at night when I'm gone. Bin-Three told her as much on the second day. Kat made her way past the room and headed for the Molucs. She wanted to make sure they were okay. The warp flipped her stomach, who knows what it did to the animals on board?

The fuzzy dragon-like creatures were curled up together in a nest of snow. She longed to pet them, her fingers touched the cold glass that encased them. *They look so peaceful.*

Familiar footsteps entered the giant chamber, and they echoed off the quiet, steel walls. Her fingers froze on the glass and the shivers that ran through her weren't from the cold. Kat took a step away from the enclosure as the thuds came to a stop next to her.

She looked up into dark, emotionless eyes, but her gaze didn't linger on them for long as they drifted down a hard, lean body covered in a white form-fitting bodysuit. The Cyborg was imposing and far too large not to be noticed, not to be frightened of and appreciated. If Dommik ever happened to fall on her, she would be crushed. She glanced down and saw the outline of a large cock, it twitched when her gaze settled on it. His body was frightening, but his bulge was terrifying.

The Cyborg cleared his throat and her eyes shot back up to his emotionless face.

"Your name is Dommik," she uttered. Her cold fingers rubbed her cheek as the Cyborg studied her.

"And yours is Katalina." He turned away as she blushed. The outline of his ass came into view and she had to stop herself from reaching out and touching it.

"Call me Kat."

"Don't care." He handed her something long and black.

Bastard. Her eyes narrowed as she took the item from him. It was a jacket, military quality, and sized for a large male, not her small form. The coat was heavy and rough in her hands.

"What's this for?"

"Put it on. We're about to land and return the Molucs back to their homeworld." Dommik dismissed her as he turned to the console next to the glass unit and typed. His long fingers danced over the screen. "Make sure you watch my every move so you can add it to your next report."

Bastard.

Kat shuffled on the thick jacket, dwarfed by it, consumed with the smell of metal. Gravity shifted under her feet, briefly disorienting her. The androids operated a device on the other side where part of the

Moluc's enclosure began to fold in on itself. The creatures shifted and uncurled, waking up, fluttering their fluffy wings in the drifts.

The hatch opened to a glorious white and turquoise world. Giant, crystalline snowflakes fell quietly from the sky and between the flakes she saw a flock of Molucs flying in the distance.

"Are they going to be okay?" she asked.

"Yes, they'll start their own flock. They're a mated pair and the female is heavily pregnant."

She walked over to where the creatures were being ushered. "Bonnie is pregnant?" How had she not noticed? It wasn't like she hadn't stared at the dragons for hours desperately wanting to cuddle them.

Dommik stepped up behind her. "You named them?" The glass enclosure shut and the snow inside began to melt away.

Kat watched the dragons cover each other with their long, white wings. "I named them Bonnie and Clyde."

"Attachment grows when you give things names." He turned toward her. "They mate for life and no other Moluc would approach a bred female, regardless. They are herbivores and very territorial of each other." Dommik looked down at his leg as a knife appeared in his hand, and he strapped it to his thigh.

Kat flinched as a freezing gust of wind hit them. Her curls flew back in a mess of webs around her head. "I wish everything bred for life, a life-mate, or such. It would make the world better." She shoved her hair out of her face.

Dommik stepped between the opening and her, blocking out the wild wind that wanted to freeze her skin. "Unless your soulmate turned out to be evil, a murderer, a drinker of the blood of innocents. Or a rapist. A system like that wouldn't differentiate." He took a step closer to her and Kat felt the cold breath in her lungs seep out through her parted lips.

A tingle, slow and steady, drifted down her body and settled between the crux of her thighs. The Cyborg, with every hard muscle outlined, moved a hairsbreadth in front of her. His thick black hair fell between them, a soft whisper would shift the silken strands.

He looked down at her, towering and deadly. Only the heat coming off his body touched her now, an invisible force-field to the elements.

"Evil people may be paired together?" Kat kept her eyes on Dommik's dark ones. Her nipples pebbled against her shirt; she sucked in her stomach and lifted her chin. Caws and high-pitched cries rose from the Molucs, their excitement at being home evident in their raucous frenzy. "Maybe we shouldn't paint everyone as black and white. Some people lose their way and that one person was meant to bring them back."

A twitch of a smile hit the Cyborg's lips. Kat leaned into him, intrigued by the show of emotion. She knew better, she didn't even know the man, but she couldn't deny her attraction to him.

He lifted his hands and tugged the lapels of her jacket. Startled, she watched as he zipped it up to her neck only to tug the hood over her head. Long, white fingers, painted metal in their strangeness, tied the hood at her nape.

The Cyborg leaned forward until their faces were an inch apart. Kat thought he might kiss her, and the need to stay and feel his mouth was almost as strong as her need to run and find a weapon.

"Good thing there's no such thing as fated mates," he whispered, his breath hit her lips. Kat shuffled as the ache built at her core. An ache that badly needed to be soothed.

His nostrils flared and his face darkened. Dommik jerked back with disgust on his face. He turned from her and strode toward the exit.

What did I do? Do I smell bad? She looked down at herself dwarfed by a jacket that reached her knees. Kat glanced up just as he walked out into the wind and swirling snow.

Kat called after him, "You can't go out there in just a skin-suit! You'll freeze."

"Make sure you get all of this in your report," he grated back at her as the hatch closed behind him. The Cyborg vanished in the white.

She looked around as the wind was cut off and everything went quiet. Two androids were inside the glass cage, cleaning it. She wrapped her arms around herself feeling her skin prickle from the heat and the cold and the betrayal of her body tingling with desire.

Eventually, the heat left her and she was just a shivering stick.

The androids finished up what they were doing. The Molucs' habitat closed up with all traces of the furry creatures gone. Kat felt alone. She didn't know

57

why she stood there and waited until it occurred to her she was waiting for Dommik's safe return.

Bastard. It wasn't her job to wait on him or for him, even if her life directly depended on his.

"It might come for you too, Kat. You'll have to be strong now waiting for it, and even stronger if it comes for you."

She was always waiting, and had been ever since her birth.

Her parents had been doctors and like all doctors had followed the Hippocratic Oath. *'I will do no harm...I will prevent disease whenever I can, but I will always look for a path to a cure for all diseases...'*

They had met in the civilian medbase outside Gliese while the settlement of the off world colony went underway. It was once a military base during the great war against the Trentians, but now it was a growing homeworld for half-breeds. Earthian and Trentian couples, ruled by both species and the appointed representatives that lived planetside.

Kat sighed and walked back toward the console room. The drag of the jacket flapped against the back of her knees.

Her parents had contracted a parasite from a local food source on the planet. It stayed dormant in their bodies, living and growing in their intestines, invisible and alien. When her ma got pregnant with her, her parents made their way back to Earth.

Kat was going to be an Earth-born human. They wanted unrestricted access for her to go to the best universities, the best hospitals, the best *'Earthian'* everything. It wasn't until her mother was in her third-trimester that something went wrong. She started to form blisters all over her hands and feet.

When she was delivered, her mother never recovered; she only grew worse. First, it was the blisters, then nausea, body aches, and insomnia. Her father started to show symptoms too and it was then that a group of officials seized her parents and herself and placed them into quarantine.

Kat was too young to remember much. She only had vague memories of doctors with white masks on and her grandmother's musings. Sterile rooms and small spaces.

The parasitic outbreak was streaming on every channel back then and doctors from all over the universe, Trentians and Earthians alike, came together to save their sick people. They eradicated the species that carried the parasite, ensuring no new people would unknowingly get infected.

Many people died because there was no way to cure it once the symptoms began to show, and everyone else was forced to take a vaccine.

She had watched her parents bloat and boil until they eventually popped like the blisters that started on their feet, her childlike eyes shielded from them only by a glass barrier. Her father had curled his body around her mother's corpse as black mucus dripped from his nose.

The doctors took her away from that world and kept her in quarantine for years. But she exhibited no signs of the dormant, microscopic parasite.

Kat had learned a lot back then, she learned how to take her own blood, run the medbay machines, test her own urine. By the age of seven, she could change her feeding tubes and run the physical exertion tests, her toys replaced with medical equipment.

When she turned ten, her grandmother won the case for her guardianship, but there still wasn't a cure for the Gliese parasite. Only a preventative treatment, a shot filled with nanoparticles that cleaned out the system, and it worked for all illnesses but was only temporary. So Kat was released from her white prison and from the impersonal doctors, her medical toys, and into a world filled with metal and green, blue-grey skies, and water that fell from above. A world where the temperature couldn't be regulated and where food wasn't served in packets.

Kat took the preventative shot right after her grandmother died. Her fingers came up to rub the spot on her arm.

Her grandma caught the parasite. From Kat herself, no doubt, and it was still uncertain how it transferred to the woman. She had been with them from the beginning, always on the other side of the glass barriers, a constant fixture in her granddaughter's life although distant and far.

It wasn't until her grandmother had first wrapped her in a hug that warmth entered her childhood.

But Kat could never stay away from the cold, crisp, sanitized rooms of the medical facilities and when she got her GED online, locked in her paisley-splashed room, she went for her nursing certificate. She wanted to think it to honor her parents, but deep down her reasons had been selfish. It was comforting to her in a nostalgic way. The way only childhood memories could be.

Maybe she was a little crazy, evidence with her being on a Cyborg's ship alone, god-knows-where in space, surrounded by stark conditions that were only differentiated by darkness, and an unknown amount of androids.

A message popped up on her screen. Mia.

Kat sighed and without reading it first, began relaying her observations of the day. Complete with seeing the icy planet and the Molucs. She referred to them as Bonnie and Clyde for her own satisfaction.

The tips of her fingers swiped over the smooth keyboard, numb from the brief opening of the hatch. She slid her hands into the long arms of the jacket and brought them to her lips, eyes closed and her body tense. Her breath warmed up her cheeks.

Her body had just started to thaw when the flash of a new missive appeared on the screen, catching her eye. Without her interference, it opened up and the blur of a video-feed came on. Her eyes narrowed as a man's face appeared through a haze of static and a struggling connection.

Kat noticed the tattoos first. Guns on both cheeks pointing toward his mouth, numbers below his eyes that looked like code and hair buzzed off in a military cut.

The man flashed his teeth. "You must be the EPED spy."

She should have been wondering how he could see her through all the static, but instead she blurted, "I'm not a spy!" Kat's hands fell from her face.

"So Dommik caught himself a girl. The word has gotten around that he had a human on his ship."

Kat tried to exit out of the video-chat, but her screen was frozen.

His laugh came through with fuzz that grated on her ears, gleeful and menacing. An android stepped into the doorway and stared blankly at the exchange. Kat looked at it, knowing it was reporting to Dommik, and the lights over its face flashed. Kat looked back at the video-feed.

"Who are you? What do you want?"

The man smiled and sat back, his foot braced on his knee. "I wanted to see for myself if the rumors were true. Dommik likes to trap his victims."

"I'm just doing the job I was hired for," she said but now did feel trapped. "Who are you?"

The guns on his high cheekbones expanded as his smile grew wider. "Let's just say I'm a co-worker. A fellow EPED employee. Tell me, how did you talk your way onto his ship?"

Kat pursed her lips. "You're not working for Mia are you?" Mia had asked that same question and she kept asking it every time Kat made a mistake.

The man let out a shrill laugh. He leaned toward the camera until his tattooed face filled up the feed. His eyes were white-washed, almost as if he were blind with a moldy glare to them. "Mia has her way. She's desperate, that one, but not desperate enough to talk to me."

Curiosity killed the cat. Or Kat in this instance. "Is it because of the guns on your face?"

The man flashed his teeth at her and for a moment they were sharp and canine. "I can put guns on your face, babydoll, or I can put them elsewhere."

62

She couldn't stop the disgust on her face. She tried again to unfreeze the console even though a large, sharp grin filled her screen, at the corner of her eye. Kat could see it clearly but refused to look at the man dead-on.

"You should ask him about the roaches. Ask him about the webs."

Kat didn't realize it, hadn't heard the tell-tale footsteps or the hum of the hatch opening, but the next moment her chair skidded back and her hands flew to the armrests. Dommik, in his white suit once again blocked out the view she wanted and didn't want to see.

"See you in Ghost City, friend."

Chapter Six:

· · · ·

Dommik turned around to see the girl swivel in the chair, her mouth parted in a gasp. Kat was still wrapped up in his jacket, hands disappeared into its sleeves, the hood still tied at her neck and framing her face.

If Gunner had seen her wild tendrils, he wasn't sure if he could keep the other Cyborg from her. Gunner was created much like himself but with a different set of DNA and a different skeletal model under his skin. Dommik questioned who was more of freak: himself or Gunner, who had Jackal in his veins.

Marking and fucking and scavenging everything he set his eyes on.

Gunner was banned from government-protected areas even though he worked the same job as Dommik. Stryker took his loads to port for an additional fee. It was a win-win situation for the people they worked for: they didn't have to deal with Gunner, and Gunner got to keep his job and remain in the shadows.

"Roaches?" she asked, as her hands came out and untied her hood.

Of all the things she could have asked him. The invasion into his personal life, his quirks were no one's business but his own. Dommik kept ahold of his restraint despite the anger burning through his veins while the animalistic part of him vibrated from

64

within. Gunner had a way of making everything more complicated.

Dommik never wanted another human on his ship, had made sure he took every measure to garner the trust of the government and the EPED and now they demanded more than he wanted to give.

Her hair came free as the hood dropped around her neck.

He took a step toward her. His control splintered. He imagined her in nothing but his jacket, naked and shivering underneath as he slowly unzipped it from her body. Revealing her to his eyes, his hands, and his dick, inch by inch.

The metal plates in his body began to shift. The thing that made him something else. Something different. Dommik stopped, watching the girl's eyes grow wide, a wince of fear, and the silence that followed when all one's air was exhaled from their lungs.

She checked him over. He stood up straighter. Kat shuffled in her chair.

The smell of her arousal hit him like a jackhammer and all thoughts of Gunner fell away. His nostrils flared.

He had scented it before with utter confusion, with the wind at his back, drifting the perfume away from him. Now he didn't have the breeze and the snowdrifts to which he could escape. He only had his control. The smell grew stronger under his stare, his eyes locked at the covered crux of her sex. Her body adjusted, readying itself for his invasion; his cock jerked in response.

She wants me. Dommik burned and tempered.

"Do you like them?" he asked her, his lips flattening. He would ensure her disgust replaced the dew between her thighs. The truth often did that.

"Does anyone like them?" Kat made a face. "They carry disease and they infest. They're resilient against most methods of pesticides." She tugged the long sleeves of his jacket up her arms. Dommik clenched his fists. "And they're impossible to get rid of. Why? Does this have something to do with the man on the console?"

"It has nothing to do with him," he shot out. Why bring him up? Was her arousal brought on by his guns? Had he misread her attraction? "Hope, Katalina, you never encounter him again. He would have you on your knees and no other way."

"He said he was a co-worker. Who is he and how did he freeze your systems?" She tried his patience. But that helped restrain his ardor. Dommik walked to the door, knowing Kat would follow him. He kept his pace slow so she stayed near.

If she wants to know about the roaches, I'll show her the roaches.

They ended up at one of the many sealed doors around the large room. Each door held its own secret and those secrets now slept during the work shifts and now only got air time at night.

He looked back at Kat. "He has nothing to do with you, but if you are so desperate to learn more, I'll invite him over for dinner," he snarled.

Her lips twitched. "Let me guess? I'll be the food?" She let out a soft laugh. "Boy, would he regret eating me." Something shifted in her voice and her brief mirth was replaced with sadness. "Invite him

66

over for dinner and we'll see who has the last laugh. Do Cyborgs eat?"

Dommik typed in a code and the door shot open. He stood in the doorway and challenged her to go through.

"We do eat."

The light turned on and hundreds of creatures scurried about in confusion.

Her reaction was exactly what he had anticipated, down to the parted lips and hushed inhale of breath. She glanced at him then glanced back at the white room. Sterile and utilitarian with smaller glass enclosures throughout. *Smaller cages*. They did the same thing as the large ones but for an entirely different purpose. The girl walked past him, her arm brushed against his stomach and entered his "hobby" room.

Kat spun toward him as the door closed at his back, green eyes that cut through his, wide and shocked. "You EAT roaches?"

Dommik let out a laugh. "No."

"Thank God."

The smell of her arousal was gone, filtered out through the sterilization system, and it wasn't replaced. He felt its loss, but it warred with his goal to keep her cold.

Why take what she would regret giving? He leaned against the closed door and watched as she tiptoed through the chamber.

When she made her first lap around the room and passed him by without looking his way, he asked, "What do you think of my pets?" He rubbed his mouth, waiting for her answer. And it wasn't because

67

he asked her a question...but because he cared. The bugs were contained, but they still created a festering image within their capsules. They were countless now within the cases and they belonged to him, not the EPED, but him.

"I don't like them."

"Is it–"

"–I pity them."

Dommik crouched in the corner and watched her. His arms settled over his bent knees. "Why?" *Pity the most evolved and interesting creature in the universe?*

"You have them stuck in here against their will."

"Roaches don't have a will."

"Everything has a will. Why else would they eat and breed? And seek out places that protect them from humans? They evolve because they have no other way to survive."

"I thought you didn't like them?" he smirked.

"I don't. They carry disease." She stood before the tubular glass that contained the largest species he owned.

"Not all of them do. Roaches can survive a week without their head. They can be submerged underwater for over thirty minutes and not die. They are the Cyborgs of the bug species. There are, in fact, Cyborg roaches spying and crawling around Earth, each its own intelligent creation of mankind."

Kat turned toward his crouched form. "You can survive without a head?"

"Absolutely. If I upload myself into another tech source first."

"And breathe underwater for that length of time?"

68

"Not me, personally, but other Cyborgs can survive weeks underwater," Dommik answered as she walked out of his line of sight and was obscured by a hundred twitching bugs. Even amongst the obstruction of the critters and the curved glass, her emerald eyes glittered like beacons and her copper curls reflected off the clear surfaces.

She looked at him through the curved glass, her features disrupted, ugly, and appealing all at once. "So. You're telling me that you're more roach than human? And why? Expecting me to be disgusted by that?" Her lips turned down in thought. Kat looked at the bugs with glass-filtered beady eyes. "I don't even know you. Why do you think I would care?"

But she wants to know me. You're obvious, Katalina. You just don't realize it. Dommik thought about that because in its grim way, he was doing the same thing, and he was being more obvious than her.

Her head popped out at the side. "Why do some of these have colors? Are bigger? I've never known a species of roach that had a blue antenna." She looked away from him and back at the cases. "I've never seen roaches look like any of these before...except those," she pointed to the last case in line. "Those look like the ones I'd see in my grandma's garden."

Dommik got up and walked over to her, pleased with himself and for her observation. Girls didn't like to know about bugs, but she knew enough to know that the ones before her were not entirely right.

There were six enclosures in total and he started with the one she stood in front of. The *pretty* ones. With the blue appendages. "It's because these aren't from Earth." He indicted them. "I found this species

69

on Elyria when out on a mission. I didn't think much of it at the time, but as I continued to hunt, I realized something."

There was a pause before she spoke. "What?"

"That I had seen something like it before. I was almost gored that day, fuck, it took over my processors until I captured my prey and sealed it on the ship. I went out to look for the bug. Three days of searching before I found it again. I brought it aboard to run a series of tests. Do you know what I found?"

"That it was a roach?"

"It shared enough DNA that, for the first time, I couldn't logically find an answer. Within myself or within the network."

"What if humans brought it to Elyria on accident and the environment changed it?"

"I thought of that but no, enough of it was different that it wouldn't have been possible to evolve in such a way in such a short amount of time."

"Radiation?" she asked him, her eyes trained on the bugs.

"Did you grow up on cartoons?" They glared at each other before he continued. "I found more and kept them to study and compare. It wasn't until several years later on a mission to Taggert, to fight back the monsters that tried to break open the prison that I found these," he indicated the second enclosure closest to the door in the room. A roach that was small and beige, light and sandy in its color, designed to blend into the wastes of that world. "I captured a handful and brought them aboard. They shared DNA with the roaches from Earth and Elyria."

70

Kat cocked her head and studied the new roaches with interest. "That's not possible," she whispered after a time.

"Is it?"

She looked up at him and threaded the hair back from her face. Dommik's internal mech ground against each other. The inhuman parts of him wanted to take over and unleash on the girl that gazed at him. No matter what he told himself, he knew he was no better than Gunner or any other man. It had nothing to do with his urges but more to do with his restraint, which had never been tested as such since his youth.

The scientists in the cybernetics lab had tested him and every other Cyborg like him against their basic animal instincts. First food, then territory, shelter, space, and finally the need to breed.

They didn't need any more rapists in the field during wartime. Not to mention, more than half of his doctors were women and knew better than to send super soldiers out into the field without knowing that aspect about them.

Their *mothers* made sure they knew how to behave like all mothers should. As far as Dommik knew, no Cyborg has ever forced him or herself on a victim. And he wasn't about to be the first.

Kat looked away from him. "I don't know. I didn't study history, space law, or hard science." She admitted. Her arms sunk back into the long sleeves.

"What did you study?"

"Nursing. It's in my file. I studied hospice care," she whispered, "to take care of the dying."

"And you walked onto a ship that holds life and death in its hands."

71

"It was that or tea."

Dommik studied her, confused. He wasn't prone to be curious about humans, but the twinge to ask her to explain herself was felt in his gut. He would have to meditate on it later...or consult his brethren.

She went on, "What about the others?" Changing the subject and walking to the next glass.

"Those are from Gliese." The girl stiffened, furthering his curiosity. "I saw them when I was stationed there during the Great War. I only went back for them recently."

"They also have the same DNA?"

"Yes."

He could hear her heart speed up, elevate, pulse rate erratic. He watched her staring at the bugs. Her delicate hands lifted up to plaster themselves on the glass. The roaches twitched and scurried away.

"Truly. The same?" she asked again. The heat of her hands created a weave of condensation.

"Yes."

So many emotions flashed across her eyes that he couldn't pinpoint one. Her face was blank before it was sad until it turned to stone. The need to reach out and touch her was great, but his metal muscles remained stiff at his sides. He saw his doom in her eyes.

Kat absorbed the roaches, her body in profile now, and if he wanted to, he could reach out and touch her in less than three strides. He could have her in his arms in a second.

"How similar?" she asked. Her hands dropped and vanished back into the jacket's sleeves.

Dommik shrugged, "As similar as the rest."

"Have you encountered any other bugs on Gliese?" She continued to study the black roaches from that planet, a faraway look in her eyes. He looked at the critters that held her attention.

"Many."

"Do you have them here? On the ship, like these?"

"No. I only study roaches." He watched her watch the bugs. Her body heat fogged up the glass case. Eventually, her mouth puckered and she took a step back. "Why?"

Kat finally looked back at him, her face softened with worry.

Dommik stood up and stepped toward her. He asked again, "Why?"

"My parents were doctors stationed on the orbiting medical center," she trailed off, her fingers twitched at her sides. "They met there and went planetside in rotation and did fieldwork for the base and new colony efforts. When they conceived me, they returned to Earth so I wouldn't be labeled as an 'offworlder.'"

"And they brought bugs back with them?"

She took a deep breath. "You could say that."

Dommik pressed a button on the panel next to them, directly under the glass enclosure of the Gliese roaches. The panel popped open to reveal a filter contraption and debris from the creatures above. He indicated a button off to the side. "Food. It's now part of your job to feed them daily and clean out the waste." Dommik walked to the door and it slid open soundlessly. "If you have any questions, ask one of the Bins."

She called out after him, "What about the reports?"

He closed his eyes only to open them slowly. The EPED didn't know about his hobbies and he would like to keep it that way. But he wouldn't ask her to lie for him on his behalf. "It's your choice."

A soft sighed, "okay," was his only answer.

Dommik turned back toward Kat, her body and her eyes far away again. "It's not uncommon, you know, to accidently bring back things to Earth. Or to any other planet." He wasn't sure why he needed to say it, but he felt the odd need to console her. "It can't be helped. Mistakes happen."

"I know," she murmured, glancing his way.

"That's where I come in, Katalina, I help prevent these mistakes, mitigate them, contain them. It's why the Earthian Planetary Exploration Division exists. I might only be the one that captures the *snake*, but those in the background use that snake to create the anti-venom."

He left her at that.

Chapter Seven:

·····

Days passed in a quiet, vacuous haze. Kat had no sense of time anymore. Only the ushering of Bin-Three to take her back to her quarters at the end of her shift and the android waking her up each morning with a bland protein bar.

What she did have to tell time was reports, wrappers in her waste receptacle, and the lengthening of her nails. She could have looked at the date on the network, but time seemed meaningless when stuck in a small space with no eyes on the skies. No eyes on space.

She had not seen Dommik in days, not even in passing, and her need for human contact was beginning to grow strong. She could deal with no contact with the outside world as long as the loneliness was interjected with other people. It was almost comforting to recreate a fantasy of her childhood. But this fantasy came with androids and monsters rather than doctors and nurses.

Kat curled into a fetal position on her cot, tugging the cloth blanket up to her mouth. Today was a rest day and although she had nothing better to do than study diagnostics on the screens and the creatures onboard, this morning she was going to take it slow. She sighed into the covers.

Twice now, new species had appeared in the menagerie, and she knew it was all happening late at night while she was asleep. Dommik was avoiding her and doing his hunts at night. It perturbed her that she had slept through two landings, missed two worlds, with no knowledge of it.

So now she tried to keep herself up at night. Only to perceive nothing, not even the heavy footsteps of the Cyborg lurking in the passageway.

She was determined to be awake the next time the ship landed.

Except I need sleep too.

A ping sounded at the door. Kat shifted her head to look at it and willed the android to go away. Her eyes narrowed and began to close when a knock accompanied the ping. Whoever was outside her room was adamant about making themselves obnoxious.

The sound followed her as she jumped out of bed and peeled the curls stuck to her cheek away from her face. "I'm coming," she groaned.

The door opened to one of the Bins carrying her morning nutrition. "Good morning, Katalina. I have brought your breakfast."

She took it and waited for the robot to leave. It didn't.

"Call me Kat... Please. It's the rest cycle," Kat reminded it.

A light flashed across its non-face. "Yes. We have expected a routine from you and when you did not follow it, the other Bins and I decided to follow up."

Kat opened the bar and bit into it. *Peanut butter.* Ugh. "I'm fine." The android turned to leave. "Bin, wait! Do you have a kitchen on this ship?"

It stopped and flashed. "We have a molecular replicator."

"Can you take me to it?"

"No. It is in a restricted area."

Kat looked at the uneaten bar. "I'm very hungry."

"I will provide you another bar." It turned to leave again.

She followed it, leaving her room barefoot and in an oversized shirt. "I need real food, Bin, please. It can't be restricted enough to stop you from taking care of me."

"A protein bar is food. I will provide you another."

It kept walking away. Kat looked briefly back at her room, the door now closed, and decided that sleep could wait.

"Check my stats." She stopped and reached out her arm. The robot came back to her. "I'm actually not feeling well at all. I think I need to go to the medbay."

The Bin jerked and moved up to her. It took her hand and the metal of its fingers heated in her grip. Kat held still as something pricked her skin and the android beeped. She had encountered her fair share of the medical mech, it was easier and cheaper to employ an android than it was to find a human routine-care doctor. A series of lasers ran up her arm and the pinch on her hand released.

"You are not at optimum. You have higher than average sodium levels and are moderately dehydrated. I will take you to medbay."

Kat hid her smile and continued to follow the robot. It led her toward the hull but stopped at a door opposite of the facility. One that had remained closed for her until now. It opened for the Bin, and just beyond was an elevator.

She stepped into the small dimly lit boxed lift, and immediately felt the temperature drop. The door shut as tiny butterflies fluttered her stomach and bumps covered her skin.

Maybe I should have gotten dressed. It was too late now. The lift stopped and opened to another dark passageway.

Kat fell in line behind the android. It looked like an exact replica of the floor they had just left. But as they turned the corner, an aura of light filtered through the hallway, and she could see a view to the stars as they walked closer toward it.

Black and white star fields filled her vision off of a side alcove with plush chairs sitting in a 'U' shape for watching it. Her stomach grumbled, reminding her to seek the kitchen, but her feet were rooted to the floor.

She could barely take in a breath and the pleas of the robot behind her went unnoticed.

Kat had been out in the open before, living in the metal and cement cities of Earth, her grandmother's sizable backyard filled with flowers and trees that glowed soft light at night. But this was different, almost painful, almost heart-breaking. She wanted to turn away and go back to her room, but her body remained rooted in place.

Her muscles tensed and her hands became slick. She bunched them up into her night-shirt.

"Ain't nothing good out there, Katalina, nothing but experience and space. Tried to tell your ma that,

but she wouldn't hear it. Young thing like her wanted to find her own way and she was determined that her 'way' was out there and not here on Earth." Her grandmother sipped her sweet tea as she rocked the swing with her foot. Nothing but dirt lay below her rocker. The grass got squished away by the soles of her bare feet. They gave up growing long ago. "Ain't nothing good here either. I'll give her that."

Kat found her footing just enough to flop into one of the plush chairs.

"Katalina Jones, you are not authorized to be there. I must insist we leave."

She ignored the android.

"You are not authorized to be there. I must insist we go to medbay," it repeated.

Stars flew by, and sadly she couldn't tell if they were meteors or asteroids.

"All the good left Earth when your grandpa passed away," her grandmother mumbled into her cup. "You're here though, that says something."

She never knew her grandfather. "I miss you," Kat whispered to herself.

"The Earth will miss you too when you leave."

She wasn't sure how long she sat there, but she vaguely registered that the android had stopped talking at some point. Her eyes were glued to the scene and her mind drifted. Kat needed to watch the universe.

It made her feel small, really small, and insignificant. And stupid. She didn't know why she was there and couldn't figure out the choices she made to get to this moment. But the one thing she knew was that it made her sad. She pressed her hands against her face and cried.

●●●●

"CHANGING COORDINATES to Ghost City," Dommik called out.

"'Bout time, I've only been waiting since our last talk," Stryker's voice came through the intercom.

"Had to make several stops on the way. You know how it goes."

"No, I don't, and I have far too much cargo for my ship to handle. I can't work when I have no room for it!"

Dommik smirked. He leaned back into his chair. "Yeah, well, I would feel the same way if I were helping Gunner too."

All he got was a grunt for an answer. He clicked his fingertips on the armrest, a spool of rope in his lap. "Is he meeting up with us?"

"Yeah. The man is a system behind me. I think he's planning to stay in the city for a while, at least until I finish this shipment and wire him his payload."

"Odd."

"A little, but who knows with him? He's just on the edge of psychotic. Maybe Brash is lodged at the city as well and he's fixing to get himself another tattoo. I'm assuming you got my payment then?"

"Yeah, and then some." Dommik looked down at the bundle of rope in his lap, his hand buckled and split in two as he picked it up and started to weave it. Rough cord slid across the metal appendages as his extra fingers unclipped from within his arm until he had three working hands. He could split his legs as well until he was nothing but a torso, a head, and a man with eight pieces. He was truly terrifying in his other form.

"An imp of a girl, I heard."

Dommik's hands crashed back together in a crunch, the rope torn into pieces and dropped to the floor.

"Who told you about Kat?"

"A kitten? Even better." Stryker laughed, but it came through fuzzy. "Mia told me. She's pissed at you."

"She has no reason to be. There's no way she was getting on my ship. I took this job with the understanding that I work alone."

"Yeah, until they can't trust you anymore with their equipment. What about the girl?"

Dommik sighed. Bin-One's electronic footprint walked up beside him, and Dommik raised his hand to keep the android silent. "What about her?"

"She's obviously there to spy on you. You gonna keep her, or drop her off? If she's registered, I'll take her off your hands. Could use a little conversation now and then. And I'm as boring as they come, nothing to tell the pegs back at base."

"What happened to your crew?" Did he want to drop Kat off at the port? He liked her, he hated to admit, and she smelled nice. Better than any other human he had encountered. He avoided her for the same reason.

"Hold up." A crash and a curse came through the channel.

"What's wrong?" Dommik leaned forward. He turned up the volume to listen in.

"Help...Ever...dead. Trapped. Anyo..." Several minutes went by in silence.

"Distress call." His voice had lost its ease.

"Are you going to answer it?"

It was quiet for another minute before Stryker responded, "No. I need to turn in these acquisitions. It's on an unregulated channel. Probably a trap."

Dommik's thoughts turned back to Kat. His feet hit the cords lying at his feet. "If you're sure... It sounded like a woman."

Would he answer it? Even if it was a trap? What if it was Kat on the other side calling for help? That was the problem about distress calls, only one in five were real...the rest were fake. And they always filled you with doubt. Doubt, guilt, death or enslavement.

"I'll relay it over to Gunner and see what he thinks," Stryker's voice went hard.

"You already know the answer he'll give you."

"Yeah, well, it'll ease my mind." The Cyborg let out a short laugh. "'Fuck it into the dirt. Shoot it twice in the temple. Make it swallow bullets. Grab their balls and make them bleed.'"

Bin-One remained as a statue at his side, except for the intermittent flashes, each flash was a correspondent between his androids...and the flashes had been picking up. Dommik glanced at the robot. It flashed again as he stared at it.

"'One and done,'" Stryker continued.

"I need to go. See you at Ghost."

"Yeah...maybe." The comm clicked off as Dommik swiveled his seat to face his android head on. He kicked the rope away from his chair. It flashed again.

"What?"

Bin-One stopped relaying and focused on him. *Am I actually being spied on? Did someone tap into my bots?* It was his first thought.

"Master, Katalina Jones is in a restricted area and refuses to move."

Dommik stood up. "How the hell did she get past one of the doors?" He focused his attention on his ship and connected to its systems, scanning the interior for her heat signature.

"She said she wasn't feeling well and Bin-Three took her stats. They were headed to the medbay when she stopped at the view lounge down the hallway." Dommik found her just as the robot said it. "Katalina Jones won't leave the area. We cannot touch her without your permission, Master." He started out of the bridge and through the door. Bin-One followed closely behind. "Do we have your permission?"

Dommik stopped and grabbed the bot by its head, lifting all 250 pounds of it off the ground. The android's head got tangled into the ropes crisscrossing and hanging from the ceiling. "You do not have permission. You should have told me the instant she was led outside her zone."

"It wasn't coded as a red, orange, or yellow alert, Master," It said easily, unhindered by its mistreatment. Dommik set the bot on the floor and took a breath.

"Tell Bin-Three to go back to work. I'll take care of it from here, and make anything to do with Kat a red-alert." He wiped his hand over his chest in disgust. "Leave. And never take her out of the zone again without my knowledge."

"Yes, Master. Registered." It moved away and out of his sight.

Dommik palmed his face, willing the headache coming on to go away. It took a lot for a Cyborg to get a headache and the events of this day were not likely to help. He didn't envy Stryker and if he had to weigh who was having a worse day, he had to put them side-by-side. Women could do that.

Kat did that to him unknowingly on a daily basis. He looked up. The ropes were everywhere above him, leading all the way back to his cockpit and they only stopped at the end of the passageway. They hung from the grates and the metal tubes that lined the walls, some in an intricate pattern and other parts in disarray. It was thick with forced webbing, all of it to fill his strange impulses. And his *need* to be surrounded in a web of his own design.

If she sees this...

Anyone who saw this either had one of two reactions: fear or confusion. A gut wrench that shivered through them. The only other person who saw this side of him and understood it was Stryker and it was only because he had his own eccentricities.

Dommik reached up and grabbed a tangle of cord. It soothed him. He ripped it from its support and let it fall at his feet. It was quickly forgotten as he made his way down the dark hallway in search of Kat.

He heard her well before he saw her.

The sound of sniffling reached his ears just as the scent of tears assailed him. Dommik quieted his steps and crept up on her, his frame invisible within the shadows.

Did she see the ropes? Is she crying because of fear?

He couldn't tell so instead he watched her. Her copper curls were bent out of shape and fell in pressed waves along her head. The bumps of slender knees could just be seen over the chairs, bent up and hugged to her chest, her face just above them, her mouth kissing one of them in comfort.

Her cries breezed away while her hands came up to wipe off whatever dew still lingered on her face. Eventually, her head tilted to the side and her hair fell to her shoulder, her breaths hushed and her heart fell into a slow rhythm.

He didn't know how long he watched her, having forgotten everything but her tears, but he knew when she fell asleep.

Dommik shrugged off his uniform jacket and stepped from the shadows, draping it across her shoulders. Kat twitched under it before falling back to sleep. He rounded the couch and sat down next to her, soaking in her scent and sleeping pants. His eyes turned to the stars.

How could he trap a girl like her within his web? Someone who was wild to him, wild green eyes that pierced him every time she lifted her gaze, wild hair that shimmered under the dimmed lights, and a smell he still couldn't place. His fingers drummed against the back of the couch, the other in his lap.

The sound of her sleeping soothed him. It was a break within the quiet hum of his ship. Dommik looked at her.

He could see her in his bed, lithe and molded into his side, he could feel her breaths breeze over his chest. He wanted to wrap her up, cage her away, make her into something he was only allowed to enjoy. His wingless fairy in his ropes.

Dommik tensed, disgusted with himself, and looked back at the view.

A moan pulled him back to her. Her hooded eyes brushed over with slender fingertips, only to massage the back of her neck. He sat silently, waiting for her to notice him, waiting for the inevitable.

"Oh." Kat jerked. He watched her. "Shit."

"Are you ill?"

She let her knees fall to the cushion, her bare feet slipped to the floor. "How long have you been there? No, why?"

"A while. One of my androids was taking you to the medical facility."

The girl fidgeted, pulling down her night shift; it barely touched her knees and even that was stretching it. Dommik had to fidget himself.

"Yeah, about that...I really hate peanut butter."

What? "I don't understand. Are you suddenly allergic to it? You have no outward signs." He perused her body, satisfied that she all but glowed with health. "It's high in protein."

"I wasn't a week ago, but if I have to eat one more bar, I'm going to scream. No! I'm going to take it out on Bin-Three and then cannibalize his parts. At this point, I'm sure metal tastes better than those awful bars." She crossed her arms and looked him dead in the eye. "Your bugs look better than those bars."

Dommik leaned back and smirked. "So you would eat anything rather than another nutrition ration?"

His smile grew wider when her eyes locked on the bulge between his thighs. He widened his legs just a fraction. A blush that looked more like a blemish spotted her cheeks. Kat swallowed but kept looking at him, at the spot that seemed to twitch and grow harder. He could have sworn she was undressing him with her eyes. *Not the reaction I expected. Please continue.*

She locked eyes with him. "You want me to take care of that?"

Dommik coughed and sat forward, running his hands through his hair. "Shit, Kat, no. I was teasing. If you're not hurt then why were you crying?" He changed the subject, but his mind was picturing something else entirely. Lips wrapped around his cock. He tried to will away his growing erection, but it remained stiff and painful. He didn't have control of his body around her.

Kat continued to pin him down with her eyes. "I would, ya know. It depends on the food I get out of it." She laughed. "It can't be worse than eating those bars."

Dommik didn't think he could get any harder, but he did. He pressed his hand over the tent he had on display and adjusted himself. "Why were you crying?" he asked again, trying to change the subject.

Kat's smile got bigger. "You don't look comfortable, Cyborg."

"For fuck's sake, if you wanted different food, you should have just said so."

"You're never around."

"Can you imagine why?"

87

Dommik looked away, collecting his temper, watching the stars. It was harder now and he was losing control. His fingers dug into the couch, piercing the fabric and destroying the upholstery.

I can smell your desire.

Kat threaded her fingers together just as her stomach grumbled. "I'm hungry."

"That's why you were crying?"

"I think it is..."

He let out a long breath, staring at her, knowing she wasn't telling the truth. People don't cry over food, not like she had. And it angered him. She was his to take care of, she lived on his ship, and she drove him up the wall, literally.

"Wait here." He stood up and stormed to the kitchen, beyond his ropes. Dommik switched on the processor and put in the first thing that came to mind. With the offering in his hands, and the smell of cheese overwhelming him, he was back at her side within several minutes.

Kat hadn't moved and he realized he hadn't even asked her what she wanted. He was feeding her and he had no idea how to do it well. He ate the bare minimum as a Cyborg.

The pizza looked like crap in his hands.

She sat up and spun around. "Oh. My. God. Is that pizza?" She climbed over the couch.

"Yes."

His eyes caught her bare legs as the shirt rode up and he missed it when it fell back into place.

"It's for me, right?" Her eyes were crazed and wanting.

He narrowed his eyes, in turn, looking down at her. "Maybe."

"I'm living off its fumes right now, please don't be a sadist."

"Don't trick my androids again. If you're sick, then be sick. I don't harbor liars. They have been reprogrammed to tell me the moment you are in distress, the second you ask to go within a restricted zone. Do you understand, Kat?" His voice hard and forceful.

She looked from the pizza to him. "But it got me what I wanted."

"Kat."

"It got me time looking out in space. I've never seen it before, not like this." She waved her hand. "It made me feel small." Her breath hitched. "But it also got me companionship and well, I never thought I would worship the pizza delivery man but wow, Dommik, you could make any woman's dream come true. You look like a fantasy."

He looked down at the pie he was holding with hands half-gloved in leather only to look beyond at his Kevlar-clad body and the nano-grade body suit that peaked out from underneath. He handed her the pizza. She wrenched it out of his hands and lifted the entire thing to devour.

"Wait a moment." He unsheathed his dagger while she placed it on the couch and cut the food into slices.

"Thank you," she giggled with him. "Want a slice?" Moaning and chewing. Her throat swallowing each bite and all at once, he was picturing her with her mouth wrapped around his dick, swallowing him down. Dommik had to stop himself from adjusting, again. The light flickered on his console, it vibrated and shot out a holographic screen.

A new mission.

He read the missive in seconds and the screen was gone before Kat took another bite. Every muscle in his body went tense and the stress of the day shot through him like a bullet. It wasn't an easy job; in fact, it was a difficult one and exponentially more with Kat on the ship. His eyes met hers.

She was watching him while she ate.

"A new retrieval," he told her, unsure why.

"Where?"

"A moon, far from here."

Kat canted her head, the pizza now forgotten next to her. "Is that...bad?"

"It's in a Trentian controlled sector. It's a small colony, a religious group shunned by Xanteaus, their god, and the main sect of their species. But they remain protected by the Trentian military force and are still subject to their laws." His stress increased. He could feel his metal interior pull apart, screaming for release. His hand split in two and he hid it at his side while keeping Kat's eyes. Dommik wanted to rip apart his ropes. He ached to do so much more.

"Bin-Three!" he yelled.

"Yes, Master?"

"Take Kat down below. Give her access to the menagerie food processor and the codes for standard Earthian food."

"Yes, Master."

Kat stood back up. "Wait, Dommik, what's wrong with this mission?"

90

"Please follow me, Katalina Jones." Bin-Three was at her side.

Dommik ignored her and turned away. He vanished into the dark interior of his ship as she called after him. His mind elsewhere. His mind on Mia and the EPED. And his anger.

• • • •

DOMMIK RELEASED HIS body. Tearing and ripping the outer layers of his armor off. Each of his arms split into two, his legs followed suit until he was an eight-appendaged abomination. A spider.

The rope was in his hands and the rough tear of it snapped as he pulled it apart, yanking it from the walls. His teeth, metal disguised as bone, elongated as his jaw expanded and broke away from his face. The cords continued to fall away as he tore them from the ceiling, climbing over them, bending the grates in his wake.

The smell of the wild-haired girl, the stench of the food, was unshakeable, although it was far down the hallway. Shreds fell around him as he crawled across the wall. His fangs filled with the strongest nano-enhanced paralytic poison in the universe, taken from the DNA of dozens of venomous creatures from around the universe.

He wanted to sink himself into Kat. His teeth and his body.

Instead, he went into a frenzy, purging the second floor of all his woven creations until his manic state exhausted itself. Until his androids came behind him and cleaned up his mess.

Dommik lay naked on the floor of the bridge and scraped the metal with his nails. Until he found himself again.

Chapter Eight:

• • • •

The ship was flying into port and Kat was awake for it. She felt the telltale signs in her belly, but she was also told by Bin-Three, her almost-constant creeper.

Kat rubbed her arms and entered the roach room, spending her time feeding and cleaning the filters of the critters. She was nervous and excited.

It had to be one of two places, Ghost City, where Gunner had mentioned, or the moon Dommik had been upset about the previous day. Either way, she was going to see it. She was awake. *It's going to happen.*

The last of the enclosures sealed, the alien bugs scattered around the strange, spiked sprout she fed them each day. It took the Gliese roaches hours to consume it, even when every inch of the plant was covered up by hundreds of them. Until the green foliage was nothing but a stick of twitching critters. They made her sick.

She looked away and thrust the debris into sanitation.

Her muscles spasmed, and she knew the ship had landed. A hum released around her and the sound of the hatch opening filled the sterile room. Kat wiped her sweaty palms on her pants and walked into the facility.

She looked around but didn't see Dommik.

Her steps faltered as a metal passageway opened up to a closed quarantine room. *That's not what I expected.* Her eyes ran across the space again, looking for her Cyborg.

My Cyborg? Kat wiped her palms on her pants again. Ever since their conversation the day before, she felt a change: not only was Bin-Three with her like a shadow but a tension in the air. It wasn't real, but it felt like it was going to pop regardless.

There were no footsteps again last night. She had been waiting for them, wanting them and dreading them at the same time. Uncertain about the need to be with him. Kat bounced on her feet and continued to wait. A consuming, breathless, wanting had taken over her and it was dangerous.

What if he did approach my door? Could I risk sleeping with him?

She had never shown signs of having the parasite. She also knew that sexual intercourse could possibly transfer it, although all studies on the illness suggested that it was neither an STD nor was it airborne. It was likely that it had to be ingested.

But how had my grandmother contracted it? It doesn't make sense. Kat still wasn't willing to notify the medical branch. She was an expert on it and her grandmother never gave any indication, never told her anything about her time in the hospital visiting and waiting on her parents, on her.

She had chosen to give her grandmother the death she deserved, the death she had begged her for, in the comfort of her own home. It wasn't smart.

Not by a long shot. She sighed.

Her love, her first love deserved the dangerous. Her grandmother had been her world.

It was what her grandma wanted. She had taken every precaution necessary to keep the house sanitized and insular with the help of her in-laws. They knew as much as she did and followed her grandmother's wishes. Although she now knew why. The sooner she died, the sooner their inheritance would come.

Hah. Kat spent the money on a beautiful funeral for her, a deep cleansing of the house, and she had made a hefty donation towards research.

There was a fair amount left.

Kat touched the key-chip in her pocket. There was also the money from the house. The salary she made from the EPED. All of it was collecting dust. Stale and unused. Even the amount she left for herself to buy a ticket off-world remained.

The money wasn't the issue that plagued her though. It was the parasite. It was her attraction to a man who was half-machine. *Can Cyborgs get sick?* The idea that she would have opened her door to him last night and offered him a place in her bed, her tiny bed that would probably collapse with the two of them on it.

The door opposite the hatch opened and she could now see a large, industrial space beyond. Dommik was still nowhere to be seen. Minutes went by in quiet. People walked in the distance. Her eyes followed them with envy.

Kat wiped her hands again and went toward the exit. The click of Bin-Three followed her. She stepped through the hatch and it didn't stop her, it didn't stop her when she went through it to the other side and stepped onto the port. It joined her on the deck.

"What is this place?"

"This is Ghost City, Katalina Jones. It's ruled by cybernetic beings."

Oh. They were in a giant docking station with a large opening at one end that led farther into the city and the rest was filled with small flyers static in the middle and dozens of passageways that resembled the one she had just come through. Each one, she assumed, led to a docked ship.

"I've never heard of it."

"It doesn't exist."

She turned to the android. "How is that possible?"

"It's a city based inside a giant planetary colonization ship, one of the originals, bought, salvaged, and upgraded by its owner. It's constantly traveling through uncharted space and only Cyborgs, with some exceptions, are privy to its coordinates. They are revoked if it's compromised."

"And this is its port?" She moved deeper into the cavernous space. Her body was a speck in comparison to the docked ships. There were more vessels than people and as she took in the high, arched walls and chrome interior her mouth went slack.

"This is part of the city. Each ship must remain open as decreed from the leader, it is a merchant hub where Cyborgs can buy and trade with one another and not be under the jurisdiction of any government."

Kat walked with Bin-Three along the railway, peering into open passageways that led to other docked ships, most empty. There were a handful of beings around, but none were close enough to talk to or discern their humanity. It was also quiet and made her want to whisper.

The lack of people reminded her of the New American Port at home. Half shut down, unused, and barricaded off. John and the tea stand.

After some distance, Kat stopped and looked back. No one followed them, no one had left Dommik's ship. *Where is he?* She cared about that, she told herself it was because she would've liked a guide, something or someone better than her android.

My android?

She told herself that he wouldn't mind that she left. *He may leave without me.* Her eyes widened in horror. But was it because she craved his company? Kat cleared her throat and kept walking toward the bowed entrance to the main ship. She looked at Bin-Three. *He won't leave without one of his Bins.*

"Will your Master be upset we left the ship?" she asked.

"He did not state the exterior as a restricted zone."

"And you?"

"I am to ensure your safety and report to him if you try and enter a restricted zone or if you are in distress. Are you in distress, Katalina Jones?" It flashed.

Kat looked around. "Kat. No." She kept walking, it kept following. They passed through the landing deck and...into another landing deck. She glanced between them. They were exact replicas. Lights and music streamed out from one of the passageways, on the opposite side from her. She saw a couple beings standing outside that area.

"Who runs this place?"

"I do not have that knowledge."

"You don't know?"

"I do not have that knowledge."

Kat headed toward the music. Someone must have noticed them because they were headed toward her. She had met one Cyborg and had talked to another. She hadn't offended a killing machine yet and three times were the charm, right? She eyed the approaching man with every step and met him halfway. He blocked her path.

"Who are you?" he asked.

She looked up at the Cyborg.

He was different and so unlike any being she had ever encountered. The Cyborg had a blue-grey tint to his skin and it appeared waxen and rounded with smooth lines. No creases, no body markings, nothing. *Strong features.* Not handsome, not cute, but huge and encased with muscle.

"My name's Kat and this is Bin-Three." She introduced them.

"You're a human." *Rude.*

"I am."

"Who are you with?" His voice rough with a warning.

Um... "I'm with...Dommik."

"He let you wander here without his guard?"

Kat licked her lips. "Yes? And I'm with Bin-Three." She indicated the android again. "It's deadly impressive when it wields a knife and spews fire."

The Cyborg looked at the android, sizing him up. Bin-Three's face had code coursing over it. Kat looked at the man and saw the same code in his eyes.

Oh, fuck no.

"What are you doing to it?" She gripped her androids arm, clutching it.

"Leave her alone, Netto. It's obvious that's Dommik's bot." Another man appeared. Another Cyborg. *Can four times be the charm?* This one had spiked silver hair and piercings. "You must not be important." He looked down at her.

Kat narrowed her eyes and stood in front of Bin-Three. "I work for him. Why am I being stopped?"

"We're just curious. It's not every day an unknown human is wandering around Ghost, let alone a girl, and one being without an escort."

Netto came to her side and visibly sniffed her. "I don't smell Dommik on her."

Kat backed up a step. "What is with you guys and smelling?" She stood up straighter. "Nevermind, I get it, you have enhanced senses. Well, do one of you know a doctor on this ship?"

"Are you ill? Hurt? I don't smell blood," Spike asked. She nicknamed him Spike. He went up to her and took her hand, his eyes went silver as he studied it. She didn't have a chance to tug it back before he released her.

"Katalina Jones, are you in distress?" Bin-Three asked at her side.

No. Am I? No. She looked at the Cyborgs before her. "I'm fine."

"Your vitals are average, little one, and your readings are standard, but if you need a doctor, we

99

have several on the main ship," Spike said. "I would be honored to escort you to the medical unit. It's not far."

Netto grumbled next to him, "I will come too."

Kat looked behind her back toward where Dommik's ship was docked, hoping he would walk toward her, but there was nobody. She turned to Bin-Three. "Is it all right that I go with them to see their doctor, Bin?"

"Are you ill, Katalina Jones?"

"No." She didn't know.

"It is unrestricted. I will follow you as ordered."

The Cyborgs eyed her, curiosity in their gaze, Spike reached out his hand for her to take it and Netto growled.

"If Dommik looks for me, tell him I am conversing with Ghost's doctor."

"Yes, Katalina Jones." She followed the two men into the ship without touching them. One walked at her side and the other a step in front of her. Kat kept looking behind her hoping for her Cyborg, but he was not around. She began to worry about him.

"What brings you to Ghost?" One of the Cyborgs asked her.

"I don't know. Something with Dommik and Gunner," she mumbled.

They both tensed up and stopped, looking at her. "Gunner is here?"

"I don't know."

Spike checked her out, she noticed–it was deliberate and slow. "You've met him?"

"I've talked to him. Why?" They started walking again, but tension filled the air. Netto and Spike both had their hands on their guns. Netto moved to walk behind her.

"Nothing. Just a surprise, that's all. Nothing for you to be worried about."

Kat narrowed her eyes at Spike's back. They went up a lift that had her clutching the rail as it shot up. Netto tried to stabilize her by taking her arm. She shrugged him away. Beings stared at them as they went past and deeper into the city-ship. She assumed most of them were 'borgs, based on their obvious lethality, but she swore she saw several humans.

They stopped at an open door and a woman appeared. The first one she had seen. Beautiful and perfect, wearing a lab coat, with long light-brown hair clipped back. She grabbed her in a big hug.

"Hi?"

"I'm so glad they brought you to me! It's all over the city that a human girl was walking around. Walking around and unattended!" The woman held her arms and looked at her. "You're adorable and young, and so cute. I have a young daughter and she has curly hair too." The woman ushered her into the medical lab. "Come in, sit on the cot over there. Do you need a drink?"

Kat was trailed by her three escorts. "Water would be nice."

"Out, all of you, out! Our matters are confidential." The woman shooed them through the door, and the android didn't move. And she knew, in that instant, that the doctor was also a Cyborg when numbers flashed over her eyes and Bin-Three left to stand outside. The door shut behind them.

A glass of water appeared in the doctor's hand, which Kat took warily.

"So what's the matter, beautiful? If you don't want bed play, I can warn the mech off. Netto is a good guy. Jayce though," the doctor waved her hands, "well, Jayce is Jayce."

Kat took a tentative sip and smiled. The pierced Cyborg had a name. "So this will be confidential?"

"Of course, sweetheart. Doctor-patient confidentiality. I rarely see humans anymore." The woman swiveled over to her on a stool. "I was created as a battlefield medic and well, once the war ended, I came here. I specialize in my kind, but I know human anatomy as well. But if you're here for a cybernetic implant..."

"I just had a couple questions. I have money."

"It's okay, no money needed. You have Dommik's android following you. I sent a message to his ship to tell him you're here."

Kat looked at the door and wondered if he would be mad. *He doesn't own me. I'm not his captive.* If he would leave her behind.

She raked her fingers through her curls and adjusted her clothes. She wasn't sure why she was feeling anxious. Although everything about this was risky. At least she could have a second opinion here without alerting medical back home.

She took a deep breath. "All right. I never planned for this, but recent events brought me here. Do you know anything about the Gliese parasite?"

• • • •

A HAND GRIPPED HIS shoulder and the force of it turned his bridge chair around.

Silver hair and silver piercings filled his vision. Dommik rubbed his eyes. "Get off my ship, Jayce."

"Your assistant is wandering Ghost with one of your androids, Spider-Man. Thought you should know before someone tries to claim her."

Dommik already knew. He had tracked her signature since they landed. "She can do what she pleases. If someone claims her, good riddance."

Jayce stepped back and allowed Dommik to rise. He walked over to his weapon cabinet and strapped a single gun to his hip.

He felt like shit, like rusted metal, his body depleted of poison and his thoughts weighed down by the inevitable. Kat kept sneaking into his head and it didn't help that the inside of his suit jacket smelled like her. He had buried his nose into it more times than he would care to admit. Or that he tugged on his cock at the same time.

If she had the mark of someone else, maybe she would stop haunting him.

"Well, I'll let Netto know then," Jayce snickered.

"The fucking bull shark?"

"The one and only. He approached her first. Sadly, I was second."

The thought of Kat under Netto filled him with jealous rage. He stormed out of his bridge with Jayce laughing behind.

He stopped. *What the fuck am I doing?* He closed his eyes and cooled his ardor.

Dommik checked on his creatures before he walked out onto Ghost.

"What kind of monsters are these?"

"Get off my ship, Jayce."

"Shit man, what's up?"

So many things. He turned to address the Cyborg. "Is Stryker here?"

"Not that I know of. Gunner isn't here either." Jayce stretched out his arms and threaded his fingers.

"What did you say?"

"Kat mentioned him."

So now they're on a first-name basis. And she's talking to them. Dommik scanned the facility, eying the shell he was currently standing in, registering all who were on board. Stryker and Gunner were perfectly and completely absent.

"Where the fuck is he?" he gritted. He turned to Jayce. "Can you locate Stryker's signal?" They all had their abilities, and many of those abilities overlapped, but his radar abilities were limited to his general area.

"Already did. He's not within orbit or the perimeter beyond."

Dommik turned full circle.

"What's eating at you, man?"

Stryker must have answered the distress call.

He powered on his console and sent him a message. He sent one to Gunner too. Dommik then returned his attention to Jayce. "Let me ask you something." He leveled the Cyborg, connecting with him, reading his stats. Jayce did the same. It was an electrical bonding, but more intimate and more thorough, and often needed to encourage trust amongst themselves in all things. If a Cyborg went deeper than an initial stat reading without allowance, it was permitted by their unspoken law to kill the perpetrator. "Have you heard of Xan'Mara?"

Jayce stiffened as he read his database. "It's a moon," he responded after a moment. "Trentian controlled. Why?"

"My next mission takes me there, to retrieve a plant, of all things. A flower." He began to walk down the railway, following Kat's weak scent. "There's a colony of aliens on the planet, a religious colony."

"Okay. Land your ship away from them."

"They inhabit most of the moon. But that's not the issue, they're protected under their Space Lords...and the EPED mentioned that the flower is sacred to them. A rarity. A myth. It's what got them involved I assume." Dommik left her trail, restraining his impulses, and headed toward the music. A ship converted into a lounge for Cyborgs that offered a place for leisure. A place to meet on neutral territory. It was a permanent addition to the main vessel.

His feet, all four of them, wanted to get his assistant back. He wanted Bin-Three to signal him. Instead, he stormed into the bar and found himself a seat in a dense corner where the smoke was heavy. Jayce sat across from him. His piercings twinkled in the neon lights that flashed in sync to the music.

"Why do they want this flower?"

"Supposedly it only *appears* to the worthy. That when crushed and eaten, it gives the being vitality and communion with the elements. It's also worn on the bride's dress during a bonding ceremony and, they say, helps with vitality and fertility. Maybe I'll bring you some back, Jayce, I've heard rumors you lack in that department." Jayce's only response was a scowl, but he knew better than to pick a fight with Dommik.

105

Dommik knew Mia had a hand in this, a retaliation of sorts. He hadn't helped the situation by denying her the job and then forcing all contact with Kat.

"I don't think your biggest problem is the flower, Dommik. I'm not a rusty, outdated shell yet so if you want advice, just come out with it. You can't take Kat to the other side of the galaxy."

"I have a lot of problems right now..." he split his jaw off and bared his metal fangs, retracting them a moment later. "And yes, that is a problem."

"Claim her, then she'll be safe." Jayce waved his silver-studded hand in annoyance. A twitch on his lips. "Or leave her here and let Netto take her swimming. It's all the same, except for the biting."

His muscles tensed as he pictured her with the *shark*. Her legs spread as a bald, bluish head bobbed between them underwater. Dommik hissed out a breath between his teeth, "No."

"Then claim her, wrap her up in your webs, put a ring on her finger, spread your cum over her body. Just do it in a way that the Trentians understand the bond. She isn't safe without it. Or put your damned jealousy in a jar and your cock in a sex-bot and leave her on Ghost." Jayce sighed. "Unless you don't like her."

"The flower doesn't fucking do anything, dammit." He didn't want to leave her here, he didn't want to take her into Space Lord territory, he sure as hell didn't want her to encounter a Knight, and he definitely didn't want to burden himself with keeping a girl who would one day find him revolting. He had so much insectoid DNA in his blood that sometimes he questioned his overall make-up.

It was easier for someone like Gunner, who had an exorbitant amount of canine in his system. Although Gunner couldn't be trusted because he let his *jackal* run rampant.

"Then refuse the mission," Jayce laughed, enjoying this.

"Can't. They'll blame Kat and fine her life, place stop-gates at every turn for her. There is too much money involved."

"You don't know that for certain. I think your decision is easier than you realize."

Jayce produced a cigar from a nearby wall receptacle, lighting it with an electrical fuse from his finger. The musty scent of honey and barnyard filled the vicinity. The smoke created a thicker haze between them, capturing the two of them in an amorphous circle until it was inhaled. Honey remained.

Dommik changed the subject. "Stryker encountered a distress signal."

Jayce took a puff. "Oh?"

"A woman. I don't know the rest."

"Eh. It's probably a trap." Jayce shrugged.

Dommik leaned back and checked his wrist-con. No response from his friend or Gunner. *Watch your bloody, rusted asses,* he thought to himself as he breathed in the second-hand aroma. Jayce offered a suck of his cigar, which Dommik took and puffed. His mouth filled with its heat, but his body began to destroy the carcinogens. Once the tingles started, he let it out. He handed the cigar back to Jayce.

"I should check on him."

"Eh."

Cyborgs filtered in and out of the lounge, most alone, some in pairs, talking. There were less than a dozen total. Dommik surveyed the scene and nodded at those who surveyed back. His console buzzed and a message appeared. It was from Bin-One saying his ship had received a message.

He connected his wrist-con back up to his ship's servers and scanned the database and comm files, thinking Stryker or Gunner was blocked from his personal, internal server.

It wasn't them. Dommik felt his metal pieces pull apart, demanding he shift. *Calm down.*

Kat was in medical.

His teeth descended again and he was at Jayce's throat in the next instant, the sharp points like needles waiting to plunge into flesh and bone, through metal and electricity. He tore his head back, pulling on the man's spiked hair.

"You didn't tell me Kat was in medical," he growled from his throat, venom at the ready, wanting release.

"Thought you knew," Jayce said calmly, smoke escaping his lips. "Doctor sent the message before I found you." The poison dripped from several of Dommik's teeth and trickled down the other Cyborg's neck. Jayce held inhumanly still as he was locked within a centimeter of agonizing pain. No one stopped the scene from happening.

What's wrong with me? Dommik thought.

He released the Cyborg and stormed out of the lounge.

108

Chapter Nine:

• • • •

Kat was silent as the medical tube ran over her body with lights and a series of mists that dried instantly on her skin. Dr. Cagley had had her change into a thin, tied back gown, as the full-body physical took place. She couldn't wait for the results, or for her heart to stop racing.

She had told the doctor all about her parents, her upbringing, and her grandmother. Before the conversation had come to a close, she was halfway through a body exam. Being poked and prodded and asked numerous health questions.

'How long have you been in space?'

'Are you on any medications?'

'Have you had sex recently?' She *had* thought about sex recently, but she didn't say that. In fact, she thought about it a lot. The dangerous appeal of her boss left her panting in bed at night.

There was something dark and fulfilling about being trapped in her small section of the ship, being denied access to nearly everything, and being visited by him on occasion.

It brought back the weird nostalgia of her childhood with eroticism. He was a becoming a bruise that wouldn't heal and she couldn't stop pressing her finger into it to test the pain.

Her eyes wandered around the medical room. It was pristine, and symmetrical in everything except the sparsely placed decorations and mundane prints on the walls. It warped her reality and she had to keep reminding herself that she wasn't on Earth. There was one oddity to the room and that was a picture of a young girl with long light brown hair. *Her daughter.* Kat returned her attention to the doctor.

The Cyborg woman, who didn't look a day over twenty, stood at her side reading a screen Kat couldn't see.

Shivers ran up her body. She blinked hard once and tried to relax only to be pulled from the stasis immediately.

"You're perfectly healthy."

Kat's eyes sprang open and the tube lifted up to release her. "I am?"

"Yep, I don't see any abnormalities or any sign of the parasite showing itself," Cagley answered.

She leaned forward and dropped her feet off the table. "So you can't tell me whether or not I have it?"

Cagley sat down and faced her. "No, I can't, and while the machine was running I was looking up this parasite. What I can tell you is that it has never remained dormant for this long, and every case associated with it had one thing in common: each subject had eaten the Nargeo plant, a species of plant that relies on outside life to grow. A parasite in its own right, a weed. It no longer exists on Gliese, but it remains in private collections for researchers and scientists. If your grandmother had this parasite, she would be the first case since your parents' generation. Which, to be honest, is highly unlikely."

"What are you saying? That I made it up?"

"Not necessarily. I think the experiences you had undergone during your childhood traumatized you, and when you saw another loved one succumb to illness, it opened up those wounds. You may have projected onto your grandmother and saw similarities in her symptoms," Cagley explained.

Kat wrapped her arms around herself. "So you're saying I'm crazy?" *Am I crazy?* It scared her. She was suddenly ecstatic she hadn't eaten anything yet today.

"You're not crazy, Katalina. You just need to let yourself heal." The doctor handed over her folded clothes. "Go get dressed and we'll continue."

She took them warily. "So there was nothing? My grandmother had blisters like my parents..."

Cagley smiled at her in that way a mother smiled at onlookers when her child was throwing a tantrum. "There was nothing, and the blisters could have been caused by an allergic reaction." The doctor folded her hands. "You mentioned your grandmother had a garden? It could be from numerous outside sources."

Kat frowned and looked at her limp clothes. "What if I show symptoms of the parasite? And I'm not making all of this up?"

"If you got the vaccine, it won't happen–"

"My grandmother got the vaccine..."

"You're fine, Kat." Cagley got up and wrapped her in a warm hug. Kat stood up stiffly in her embrace. "You need to grieve. Let it leave you," she whispered. Tears started to form in her eyes. Cagley smiled and added, "And Cyborgs can't get sick."

She gripped her clothes and pulled away. "Thank you," she murmured and headed into the attached bathroom. Memories flooded her as she tried to analyze everything that her grandmother had gone through, every occurrence and precaution they took. The way her voice grew guttural with saliva at the end, her wrinkled skin splotched in some areas while other areas were sunken and cold, and the faded look on her face.

Those last days had been filled with grief and every conversation had the urgency of being their last. Maybe she did need to move on.

Cyborgs can't get sick.

How can I move on when I'm only here because of her?

Kat looked around the bathroom, reaching behind and untying her gown, letting it fall, only to kick it away and dress. She tabbed on the sink and washed the stress off her face. A thunderous racket of a door slamming open and a familiar voice sounded outside in the medlab. Quickly followed by a high-pitched giggle and Bin-Three's monotonous voice.

"Where is she!?"

Kat dried her face and reached for the handle. It whipped open, barely missing her, to a very upset, very tense Cyborg.

They stared at each other, his eyes narrowed toward her startled wide ones.

"Hi?"

"How may I be of service, Master?" Bin-Three chirped up.

Dommik dropped his arms. "Are you okay?"

"Yes," she smiled and threw her arms around him. "There you are." Burrowing her face into his hard chest, hot and stiff, her fingers threaded through his long hair. He remained tense in her arms, but she didn't care. She only cared that he finally showed up and that he found her, cementing her back into reality, and forcing her to confront another issue. She wanted him. She wanted the Cyborg with the long blue-black hair and ebony eyes.

His hands cupped her shoulders and just as she settled in for comfort, he pushed her away. Kat retrieved her arms and looked up at him.

She expected fury, compassion, something to show on his face. She would have settled for confusion to match her own, but his face was blank and his body was stiff and even the heat of his hands dimmed.

"You should stay on Ghost." His fingers peeled off her.

"What? Why?"

"Because I don't want you on my ship." He turned to leave and strode to the crushed open door.

Kat was taken aback. *Was it because I touched him? Am I that horrible to be around?* Bile crawled up her throat, burning with acidic shock.

Cagley took her hand and smiled. "You should stay with me, Kat. My daughter will love spending time with another human."

She glanced at the pretty doctor as Dommik rounded the corner. Leaving a very upset Netto and an unresponsive Bin-Three behind. "Thank you for everything, Cagley. I can't stay with you." *The tea stand.*

Kat rushed after her Cyborg, running down the hall to his retreating back in the distance, catching up to him with a strangled breath. She reached out to clutch him but jerked her hand away, letting her fingers twitch against her palm.

"Dommik, please, you never showed up in the hull and Bin-Three said this place wasn't restricted." She hastened to keep up with him.

"Because it isn't. You're fired. Go back to Cagley." His voice deepened. "Or Netto."

"I'm not fired and you're not leaving me stranded here, damn it. Just tell me what's wrong. I won't leave your ship again," she rushed out.

"Get Netto to take you back to Earth."

"I don't want Netto. Dommik, I want you." He stopped and turned to face her. "Please don't leave me here. Everyone I care about leaves me..."

He studied her; she could feel his eyes burning through her, and she wasn't courageous enough to meet them.

"You, Katalina, don't know what you want."

Kat looked up. "I'm not a child or a liar." The sound of Bin-Three's metallic footsteps caught up within the tension between them. "I really want you." To prove it she balanced on her toes and placed a soft kiss on his jaw.

Dommik's hand clutched her hair and jerked her up within a hairsbreadth of his lips. She felt the thrill of his mouth moving a whisper above hers. "Think really hard, Katalina, because I don't believe you," he said softly, a warning on the edge of his words.

"Dommik, please."

"We're going into Trentian airspace."

"Okay." *Please kiss me.*

Kat was lost in him before she realized it. She swallowed and relaxed, letting him hold her up, torturing her with an almost kiss. Her neck strained as he held her in place, as her toes barely kept her standing.

Her eyes drifted from his to take in his face, the white pearlescent skin, the thick black eyelashes that blotched his equally black irises. She caressed him with her gaze, tracing his jawline, to his hair that fell in waves to frame it. The crux between her legs ached. Her hands stayed at her side.

He stood there, doing nothing, staring at her as if he had turned himself off, as if he were nothing more than a statue. A machine with nothing to power it.

"Dommik?"

He released her and she fell back onto her heels. The cold air of the ship breezed over her heated skin, cooling her desire down.

"You'll do exactly as I say from here on out. If you don't, I'll drop you off at the nearest port and leave you. You have one last chance to stay here on Ghost." His fingers swept a strand of hair from her face. "Do you understand?"

"Yes."

"I won't have you burden me. If you step on my ship..."

He turned and brushed her off, like a speck of dirt, and left her where she stood. Kat flushed speechless, choking down her embarrassment, and didn't watch him leave. His retreating steps roared in her ears. She leaned against the wall.

There was a warning and she heard it loud and clear. Could she do it? She bared her feelings to him, had told him she wanted him. There was nothing left to armor herself with and whether he chose to take her or not, Dommik would always have that power over her.

Kat pushed away from the wall and wetted her lips.

When she was ready, Bin-Three led her back to the ship.

The Cyborg with the silver hair and piercings nodded as she walked past.

She knew she was being watched, tracked, and monitored. It was like the devil himself was feasting on her mortification. When she walked into the hull, the hatch closed behind her, and the ship rumbled to life.

"Katalina Jones, we are taking off, please watch your balance." The clang of detaching metal muffled through the barrier. It settled a moment later.

Tight, large hands grabbed her from behind, she shrieked not because she was startled, but because there were four of them.

Chapter Ten:

. . . .

Kat was lifted off her feet and trapped in a four-
armed embrace. She struggled to turn around to see
her attacker, but her limbs were held firm. Familiar,
white fingers ripped into her clothing as she was
carried into a glass enclosure. The usual bright lights
of the menagerie dimmed down to the same gloom of
the rest of the ship.

"Four hands," she struggled out, flailing like a
fish against a hard chest, it burned her back and as she
slowly stopped struggling, the outline of a very large
erection pressed into her back.

"Keep moving, Kat, it feels good," Dommik
purred into her ear. "Remember I gave you a choice."

His voice tickled her skin, causing goosebumps to
prickle down her restrained arms. Her body flushed
with anxiety.

"I thought..."

"You thought what?"

"I don't know. I thought you didn't want..." She
shook her head while her focus was still on the
anomaly of the extra pair of identical hands. And they
were identical, down to the same creases and color.
"You have four hands," she announced lamely.

He loosened his grip, flexing all four of them in
front of her. She reached out and touched them only
to spring her fingers back.

"You can touch them," he said, his lips still on her ear. Kat slipped her palms over the forearms that weren't clothed, petting the smooth skin and testing it under her fingertips. Dommik's extra limbs were harder than his normal arms, although she had yet to see or feel them under his suit. They were warm to her touch, straining with their own tight tissue, but when she squeezed them, she felt metal directly underneath. Kat grabbed the wrist of one of his other limbs and squeezed to find muscle and tissue.

"So they're not the same." She faced him. His clothing was pried open and pulled tight to let his new arms free, Kat wanted to look under his Kevlar and leather to see where the new limbs came from but was hindered by cloth. "I didn't know Cyborgs could change their form."

"I'm different, a subsect, there's a handful of us and the only similarities we share are our cybernetic make-up and our *unique* design." He tilted his head. "Netto, for instance, has extra parts to help him swim and dive deep underwater."

Kat found two of his hands and brought them to her face. "What do your extra arms help you do?" His fingers elongated and shifted as she watched, transfixed until they didn't resemble anything human anymore, but one giant jointed spear. All four of them were now long daggers, sharp and double-clawed. A weapon. A frightening one.

"They help me pin things down," Dommik flexed them and trapped her against the enclosure. "They help me climb. The claws at the end secrete poison." Kat held her breath as he leaned into her and whispered, "My teeth do too."

She felt more than she heard the metal transforming along her cheek. It pressed into her skin, hot and just a little bit wet. It was the only place Dommik touched her and that small spot became a pinnacle; all of her focus was on whatever part of him pressed against her skin. What felt like a tongue glided over the bump of her ear. Hot and horrible.

Kat shut her eyes. Teeth, pointed teeth scraped down her jaw and over her neck, under her ear lobe, as his wet tongue followed suit. Her body shook with need.

It was exhausted; she was exhausted. Her mind was spinning and yet her core yearned to be touched and be filled by him. Kat wanted him inside her, at least a part of her wanted it so much that she throbbed.

Hair slipped over her arm as Dommik gnawed on her pulse with a mouth that had no lips.

"I want you, still."

"I can smell it." One of his hands turned back, cupped her sex and squeezed, while she squirmed and clutched onto him. "I could smell it on the other side of the ship. How wet you are. How wet you are for me..." He began to knead and massage the area between her legs and the more he did it, the more her essence spread. His teeth stayed on her throat like a threat as he forced more out of her. "You chose this."

He pressed her back against the glass as she dry humped his hand, the other three held her in place. Kat danced on him, sliding up and down. "I chose this."

Cyborgs can't get sick. Cyborgs can't get sick. Cyborgs can't get sick.

119

She stiffened. "Dommik, you can't get sick, right?" she asked, as he continued to play with her. The side of her throat slippery with saliva, his tongue and teeth left her, and when he moved away to look at her, his face was familiar. A face that was darkened by the shadows and resembled a skull. "Cagley said you can't get sick."

"My body would fight off and destroy any pathogens I don't want in my system. I can only get viruses."

"Viruses...like colds?"

"Computer viruses."

"What about parasites?"

"Same as pathogens. Why?" he asked, with his hand still milking her into a slow-boiling frenzy. Kat put her arms around his neck and kissed him.

His lips remained stiff under hers and his hand faltered between her legs. It didn't deter her and as she licked the hard line of his mouth and her teeth came out to nip at him, she feasted on the taste of it all.

Musk and man. Metal and mint. And she could have sworn a hint of sweat.

Kat pressed her body up into his until she was fully covered, working her way inside his open shirt. He couldn't get sick and she held onto that truth with a building frenzy. And when his lips parted, when his control came back to him, when he turned back on to respond to her, she had decided not to let him go.

Dommik would be the only machine for her.

Her back hit the wall and was pushed up until he had her at the same height as him. She clawed at him, needing to be closer, needing to purge herself of everything.

Kat whimpered when he humped her stomach with his metallic erection, pounding her body into the wall. Her mouth was filled with his tongue, thick and demanding, licking her all over while his fingers gripped her ass, groping it painfully. She was being used, consumed, and she was basking in it.

She didn't want him to stop, ever, her mind wanted to stay within the brink of this moment. Dommik was losing his Cyborg control, no matter how hard he tried to keep it, and she wanted him to lose it because if he did, she couldn't be embarrassed if she lost hers.

The sounds of thumps and groans echoed off the small space, soon followed by the rip and tearing sounds of her clothing. They were almost flesh to flesh, and Kat, wanting more, tugged on the seams of his armored suit.

Her shirt was torn straight down the middle, his nails like blades as his mouth pulled away to look down at her chest. She panted and writhed as her legs hooked over his hips.

"Please don't stop." Kat wasn't above begging, especially when he could snap her in half. "I want you so badly, it hurts."

"Wasn't going to."

Dommik's hands squeezed her breasts, pushing them together, pushing them up. He stared at the pumped up cleavage, blushed with freckles and sweat, and she did nothing but let him play. His thumbs found the tips of her nipples under the soft fabric of her bra and rubbed them, throwing her into an arching frenzy.

His erection grew and speared into her belly. She let her hand slide down his chest to cup him, finding his thick, mushroom tip pointing straight at her. Kat had never felt passion like this or such electric desire. Dommik was gigantic and her body wanted it all.

Her core ached with need, ached to be filled, and by damn...she was going to force her body to take all of him.

"I don't want to wait anymore," she mewed, glancing back up to his ghoulish face still bent down to hers. He tweaked her tits.

"Do you like this bra?"

Kat looked down at its faded blue design. "Why?"

Dommik tore the tiny clasp of fabric and it fell away. All of her clothing, besides her pants, hung limp at her shoulders. His hands cupped her again, leaving her nipples free to his gaze and to be rubbed by his thumbs.

"Beautiful, pink, and pert," he murmured, caressing her areolas in slow circles. They prickled under his eyes and beaded further, his touch heating her skin until it wasn't only her core that was soaked but her skin as well. Kat squeezed the head of his dick. "Are you ready?"

Ready for sex? "Yes," she pressed herself into him.

They locked eyes as he gently moved her hand away and unclasped his pants; they sagged on his hips, and with her help, they fell to his feet. It was then she noticed his skin-tight underlayer was a full-body suit, a second skin that perfectly outlined every tense muscle and groove on him. She swore she saw the shadow of scars on his chest but couldn't be sure in the low light.

"Let me go so I can look at you...help you peel off this layer?" she asked, lifting up to place whisper kisses on his cheek.

"No need," he groaned. He lifted her higher on the now-slick glass and adjusted his grip. "It's made with the same nanoparticles in my body. It moves and releases when I need it too," she held on as he jostled her. "I control it as well as I control my body."

"Oh."

"I'm going to fuck your breasts." His suit split open, catching her off-guard, revealing a powerful body beneath. A body built for war. A body built for sex.

A body beyond her imagination. One that could send her to her knees and beg for.

Her heart raced as she looked at him. Muscles upon muscles, scars, and violence dressed his frame. Kat couldn't see much but what she did see scared her. She was an average human girl, but next to him, clinging to him she felt more like a doll.

Her feet couldn't touch, hugging his hips. She squeezed and tried again. *I can't clasp them.* Her nails bit into his shoulders. But what was even more intimidating was that he didn't feel wholly human under her grip. There was no "give or take" with Dommik: he was a force in his own right. And as his erection sprang free, ground between their bellies, it wasn't a man's cock that poked her, but a Cyborg's, metal encased in tissue.

123

Kat didn't need to look at it to know that it was slightly curved upward and that, she swore, probably appeared more like one of his "dagger-claws," a fifth one to match his four arms.

She slipped down the glass, his hands back on her ass. "Press them together," he stared at her freed nipples, hunger in his eyes. "I'll hold you up."

Kat shivered but followed his orders, letting her hands fall to her chest.

"Don't drop me," she whispered.

"Pinch them. I want to see you play with yourself," he demanded. She pinched them, letting the tingles of heat flood her clit. "Pinch them as if I were doing it." Kat continued with more fervor, letting her body succumb to his rough voice. It washed over her, like his hands, his heat, and she couldn't get enough of it. She was burning alive, burning for him.

There was something about Dommik that she craved and as he watched her play with herself, it became clear that she had needed *this*. She needed him and for the first time felt cared *for* and not care *by*.

He moved her lower on the glass and angled her away. Her feet fell from his hip and down to grip his tense thighs. She felt safe, held up by his powerful hands, rounding her ass and the overall assurance that he exuded.

Kat pressed her breasts together as his heavy erection glided up her stomach and pierced her cleavage. The trail of precum fell hot and slick on her skin. Her ears were filled with grunts as his cock pushed her breasts apart, forcing himself into the space between them. She held on as the raw intensity

124

skyrocketed and he rocked into her hard. It was devious, wrong, but felt oh so right.

Kat closed her eyes and gave into it. His speed increased into a frenzy. His use of her, savage. His cum perfumed the air and spread across her chest.

"You've been claimed." A spurt of hot liquid hit the underside of her chin. It dripped down to coat her nipples. It made her freckles glisten.

Kat's hands moved up to grab his shoulders, her nails broke his skin as he came on her again and again until she was sticky and wet. Dommik's dick twitched with each release and continued as he laid her on the floor.

Her chest, her breasts raw and rubbed to perfection under his cock and through his eyes.

The blades of his metal fingers ripped off her jeans, taking her destroyed panties with it. She was primed, desperate for release, molten and ready at her apex. Kat smiled up at him and his still stiff cock. Dommik had stripped them both.

"You've been claimed too," she giggled and sat up, reaching to handle him.

Chapter Eleven:

• • • •

Dommik watched his trapped fairy sit up on her knees and take hold of him. Her soft smiles and impish features burned deep into his brain, his hard drives. He would forever have these images with him, tormenting him long after she came to hate him.

But his body remained stiff, needing more of her, and when her hands tugged him down he joined her on the cold ground. His seed covered her in dewy tendrils from her chin down to pool to her pelvis. The animal inside him roared; the spider inside him wanted to bind her within his ropes to feast from.

Kat was meant to be devoured. Her frenetic aura to be chained, claimed, his conquest. He wanted to capture the beauty of her, to take it with him everywhere.

She was his trophy and if another being ever sought to steal her away, Dommik would unleash a hell that the universe had never seen its like.

Her eyes flashed a brilliant, mischievous green. Pouty lips crept up into a smile, her copper curls mussed and damp around her face. He ate her up. And she touched him, her hands curved around his kneeled frame, up his tense thighs, and over his hard stomach, skipping the cock that was desperate for her attention.

Dommik didn't want Kat to hate him, he didn't want her to be afraid of him, but it was inevitable.

What he had shown her of himself was just a piece of what he truly was.

Her taste was in his mouth where he wanted it to stay.

He gripped her chin as her hands traced the scars on his chest. "Your eyes have a wicked gleam to them, Kat. What are you thinking?"

She licked her bottom lip. "I want your poison."

"Do you now?"

Her fingers tugged at his long strands, rising up to scrape her nails over his scalp. Their eyes stayed locked. "Has anyone told you that your face looks like a skull in the shadows?"

He couldn't help but smirk. "Yes. Has anyone told you that you look like a fairy?" he countered.

She shook her head as he dropped his hand. "No." Her eyes fell back to his chest. "Do they hurt?" Dommik watched as she whispered her fingers over one of his jagged scars.

"Not anymore."

Kat leaned forward and kissed them and he let her, feeling his heart sting and bleed with each press of her lips. He held still as her tongue licked the crisscrossing knife and claw marks, her lips on on his bullet markings. "I'm sorta a nurse," she smiled against his skin. "I help people die comfortably. I wish I had been around to kiss these better when you received them." Her emerald orbs caught him. "I heard kisses make hurts feel better."

Dommik's eyes narrowed. She was hurting him more than any of the battle wounds he had received before. He stiffened as she continued to worship him.

She had brought him to his knees and that floored him. He wasn't used to comforting, to passion, not at the level Kat was willing to give him and it grew in him like a weed.

His fingers caught into her tangled curls, lifting her bruising kisses away. "You chose me, Kat."

She laughed. "I think I chose you when I first saw you at the port, when you stepped out of your ship."

Dommik flinched but fought against it and took hold of her instead, his fingers white against her fiery hair. "I wish I could say you chose well." He took her mouth before she could say another word and he put himself into it, all of him. "I claim you, Katalina Jones."

And I'll scare you half to death.

She looked at him as she tried to understand his sentiment, as if she wondered if she should put stock into his words. He wasn't going to reassure her or lie to her.

Let her believe what she wants.

He pushed her back against the enclosure's floor as he covered her, and positioned her legs open. With one quick adjustment, the bulge of his cock found her dripping core and slammed into it. He roared in triumph.

Dommik arched over his fairy and quieted her gasps with his hand as she struggled and fought beneath him. He held her firm, waiting for her body to succumb, holding still as her pussy squeezed and clenched his dick. It tried to push him out, tried to fit him.

All he could focus on was swallowing her cries and how deliciously tight she was.

When her legs fell open and her muscles went pliant, he lifted up to watch as she took his claiming. He slowly rocked, finding her G-spot with his head and bumped it.

Sweat coated her freckled skin and when her mouth parted in a moan, her pained eyes hooded into submission, he pistoned into her.

He lost himself in her. Dommik held her down to stop her body from sliding up with each advance.

Each thrust brought forth his name in a moaned shriek, each pump breaking them both apart until the metal skeleton inside him wanted to rip him apart. His creature wanted to shift. Her breasts bounced, the smell of hard sex swallowed them up, and his cum remained slick on her chest.

Dommik reared up on his knees, grasping her small waist and bringing her into the new position. His little fairy gave as good as she received, gyrating her hips and finding her own pleasure. He released her, letting her take the pace, and focused on her clit. Rubbing slow and soft, quick and hard, until her body sagged and climaxed on him. With one arm snaked under her ass to hold her up, he continued assaulting her with his fingers as he took over, wallowing in her twitching release and tight sheath.

"Tired are we?" he snickered and pumped into her, forcing her body to continue.

Her eyes flickered open. "No," she gasped, sitting up onto him and enfolding her arms behind his neck. "Yes."

Dommik lost the inferno in him when she laid her head against his chest. His cock swelled and shot his load deep in a pussy so hot, so tight it could subdue him and he craved it again even before his climax ended.

He captured her in his arms and they held each other because he didn't want to let her go and her racing heart soothed him. A lullaby of life on his otherwise industrial ship.

It wasn't until Kat caught her breath and the heat between them cooled that he lifted her into his arms and walked to the lavatory.

Neither of them spoke as the water cascaded over their skin and his mark washed away. They bathed each other gently, their hands sliding over each curve and marking. He discovered where she was ticklish and she found the almost indiscernible seams where his body shifted apart.

She leaned into him and her eyelashes fluttered over his torso, the pads of her fingers wrinkled from the water fell over his muscles to caress. "I feel different."

I know.

Dommik brushed her tangled wet curls away from her face. "You just had sex with a Cyborg," he teased. "I heard it can be overwhelming."

She mumbled and burrowed closer into him. "I'm glad you can't get sick."

He looked down at her clinging onto him and powered off the jets. *Why is she fixated on illness?* Grabbing a towel from the wall, he hugged her tight within its folds, taking his time drying her skin and ruffling her hair, only wishing he had something softer to dry her with. Dommik pictured her in a bed of silk and aged flannel.

When she was dry, he picked her up and carried her back to her quarters, letting the door shut behind them. He watched as Kat moved out of his arms and rummaged through her luggage, still unpacked on the desk. She tumbled her nightshirt over her head, hiding her body from his view.

The soothing atmosphere from before vanished back into the cold metal of the ship. It was whisked away by the intermittent flashes of her personal tablet and the stiff silence between them.

It was awkward and for the first time, as he ran his eyes over her curves, he felt guilt and an unusual sense of regret. His foreplay was rusty at best, if nonexistent.

But he was also elated by the strange turn of events that put Kat and him in each other's paths.

Even now I want her. I can smell myself on her skin. The emerald jewels of her eyes caught his. *She'll always catch me.*

"Will you stay with me tonight?"

"I can't leave the bridge unattended much longer." Dommik wanted to stay with her but needed to get away. "We're headed into Trentian territory. Things will be difficult from here on out."

Her face fell and as she moved around him to climb up into her bunk, a flash of thigh had his fingers reaching out and caressing it as she settled in. She shivered.

"I don't know much about the aliens." *She masks her disappointment well.*

"Research them tomorrow." He took a step back. "And know, you're safe with me."

"I always knew I was safe with you."

Dommik nodded and turned toward the door. It opened up and he stepped out. He left so much unsaid between them, so many questions to be asked and answered but all would have to wait for another time. "Goodnight, Kat."

The door zipped closed behind him and he heard her faint response through the metal.

"Goodnight, Dommik."

Chapter Twelve:

• • • •

Things went back to normal after they left Ghost
City.

Kat woke up the next morning sore, bruised, but
well-rested with a head full of dreams. At least she
thought it was a dream when Bin-Three knocked on
her panel with a gift of real food. Her stomach
growled for the cooked eggs and fresh fruit before she
could even take the tray.

"Good morning, Katalina Jones."

"Call me Kat," she said for the hundredth time.
"Morning, Bin-Three. Thank you for the food." She
sank her teeth into a slice of apple. The food was
gone before she could truly appreciate it. But the
fresh, sweet aftertaste remained with her. Bin-Three
stayed within her doorway and watched. Kat handed
the tray back to the android. "Where's Dommik?" she
asked, quickly getting dressed and following it out the
door.

She combed out her hair with her fingers, finding
it still damp from the night before. Kat took stock of
her body as she walked. It felt well used, her calves
and thighs ached, even parts of her skin were raw to
the touch and it all brought images of the Cyborg
dominating her, touching her as if he were holding
back a piece of himself. The image expanded in her
mind until all she could focus on was the dark pitch

of his eyes shadowed by the dim lights of the ship, twinkled with the reflection of the glass.

He called me a fairy? She paused.

"He's in the gym. Should I relay a message for you?"

Kat glanced away from her body and up at the android. She had hoped he would be in the facility waiting for her. She understood those unspoken agreements about sex.

Never get attached. Never assume. Never read into it more than what was there. And most of all, don't fall in love. Love only lasts onto death and death always seemed one step behind her.

"No, thank you."

The android left her at her pseudo-office and she took her seat without looking at the empty enclosure from the night before and instead logged into the EPED server.

The afterglow of great sex and fantasy were forgotten when her belly cramped, curled up, and punched her in the gut. Kat gasped and tried to massage it away, but the ache only grew until she lifted her shirt to check her skin.

No blisters. No blemishes. What the?

She looked outside her small room, finding it empty but for one robot on the other side, cleaning the Wameck's habitat. Knowing it was cleared, she peeled off her clothes and thoroughly checked her body, the cramps growing with her paranoia. Her muscles tensed as she twisted to look at her back, running her hands over her buttocks, slipping off her shoes to look at the soles of her feet. She then rechecked every area, grimacing from the pain.

A chat opened up on her screen with Mia's name tagged at the top. It brought her out of her mania just long enough to redress and convince herself she was just getting her monthly. That she was giving into paranoia.

"Don't go looking for things that aren't there, Katalina. Leave it alone and let it rest. You're driving me crazy with how you're acting, girl."

Kat took a deep breath and dove into her work.

'Where're your reports from yesterday?'

'I'm working on them now. We had–' Kat stopped typing, wondering if Ghost wasn't known by her employers. '–stopped at a port.' She opened her backlog from the day before, finding several other messages she received. All from Mia Stavke and all in states of annoyance to demanding to downright mean. Communication with Earth or any of the bases in their solar system took time to deliver. It was like dealing with a digital pond of molasses that each missive had to swim through.

Kat pulled the data from the current creatures on board, and ran it through the division's software. Everything the androids monitored, including food intake, emotional state, chemical levels, and growth, amongst a dozen other stats were always logged. All she had to do was read it, note any shifts or changes, put in any reasons *why* the changes may be occurring and then write a visible report.

The visibility was why she was there. She wasn't sure what had happened that created the need for this job, but she knew it wasn't Dommik's approval. The living areas on the ship remained unused, undisturbed, uninhabited. There wasn't even a scuff on any of the floors... *and there are always scuffs*.

Kat finished her reports and uploaded them to the secure server, all before Mia could come back at her with another message. Her fingers paused on the keypad, debating whether it would be appropriate to ask...she was typing her question before she answered herself.

'What happened that made this job, my job, become available?' She didn't know if Mia would respond, let alone answer her, but it wasn't going to stop her from trying.

Kat flexed her fingers and attached her portable to her wrist. It could be hours, even days before she received a response and the time increased every light-year the ship moved further away. She absently rubbed her stomach as she went to the roach room.

The echo of her steps followed her. A shiver shot up her back. She shook it away and walked through the door and stopped, and waited, until the lights shot on before moving further in. It didn't matter how many weeks she had been taking care of the bugs, and the thought brought on a wave of nausea to her already invisible stab wounds in her belly: she would *not* take one step further in without the light.

When the roaches scattered behind the glass it meant they were not scattering outside the glass. Kat didn't look at them as she cleaned the debris and stuck in the plants they feasted on, always leaving the Gliese ones for last. She shredded the stalk and jammed it past the filtration system.

Her breath caught and a gag welled up into her throat, the feeling of unease returned. She hugged her body and left the gross room behind.

She walked headfirst into a familiar chest. Kat jerked back. "Sorry," she breathed as his hands cupped her shoulders, sending electrical fire straight into her, making her blush.

Dommik didn't remove his hands. "How are you feeling?" he asked. Kat looked up at him, pushing her crimped hair out of her face and lost it with a sag.

She leaned into his body and burrowed herself in his heat. "Not good."

His arms fell around her and the metal frame of him softened under her cheek until she felt cocooned, one she decided she never wanted to break out of. The cramps and aches of her body went away with each caress he gave her, over her back and shoulder blades, kneading the knots out of her neck to the base of her skull. She lulled into him and her mind went blank with pleasure.

Kat drifted off to that warm place that only an embrace can give.

"Feeling better?"

"Mmm, yes."

Is he really comforting me? Her reverie went away as he picked her up and carried her back into the ship.

"Where are we going?" she asked, tangling her fingers in his loose hair.

"Some place to talk." He leaned down and kissed her forehead as the elevator closed. Kat couldn't stop the shock her wide eyes portrayed. Dommik was hard, the kind of hard that took more than an explosive to break through, and he was quiet. She had seen him as a shadow-dwelling loner.

But now he was holding her, touching her, cradling her in his lap as he brought them to the lounge that overlooked the stars. He didn't let her go but instead settled in.

Kat stiffened.

"What's wrong?"

"This is awkward." She tried to remove herself from his lap and after a short struggle, she settled a short distance away.

"Apparently it's only going to get more awkward," he muttered, closing ranks. "How are you feeling? Really?"

Kat curled her legs under her. "I have some aches, nothing major."

Dommik's eyebrows furrowing as he stared at her. *He's reading me.* "Do you have any cramps?"

"What?"

"Cramping," he sighed, exasperated. "In your stomach."

"Yes...there is some cramping." They watched each other in stony silence, which is what every conversation and every interaction between them always came to. Quiet brooding, racing thoughts, and distrust. At least that's how it felt for her. "We had sex."

"I'm glad you remember."

"It was only sex." She stated more for herself than for anything else. "I don't expect anything from you and I know why you did it."

He sat back. "You expect your job? So, it was only mechanical for us, makes sense." He canted his head. "We are two adults alone out in space, but I think you forget Katalina, I let you back on this ship, and regardless of what happens between us, I'm still your boss and your captain. I know you're lying and I can live with that. I also know everything that happens on this ship. Everything. To what you eat for each meal, how much you eat, where you spend your time, when you step off my ship without permission, and when you send questions out to the EPED that should be directed to me. If you haven't noticed, I'm a machine and more so than most other Cyborgs out there. My ship is a machine, a machine, Kat," his voice rose, "and I'm perfectly integrated with it." Dommik took a deep breath. "This is *not* how I planned this conversation to go, but I'm curious, why did I have sex with you?"

Kat rubbed her stomach and his eyes drifted over her movements. She knew that he knew more than he let on, it was obvious, and she was aware that Bin-Three could likely have a camera on him. But they were practically strangers and when it came to his double set of arms, she probably knew his body better than the man himself.

"You said it yourself, you claimed me, and we're going into Trentian airspace. They didn't teach the nuances in school, but everyone knows they're dying out because of us and because of that, will do what they can to obtain un..." she paused and swallowed, "uninfected women." Kat looked away and out at the stars. "Which is really funny now that I think about it." She laughed.

"What's funny?"

"Nothing. I used you too, though." She turned back to face him. "You don't need to threaten me and I didn't come with you just for the hell of it." Her thoughts wandered back to the space port's entry gate. "I had my reasons." The conversation was taking a turn she didn't want to go down with him. Sex was one thing, but she knew better than to share her soul with someone, and only had several times in her life. She didn't count the doctor who only knew the pond-scum that coated the top.

Dommik watched her as she rubbed her stomach, his eyes boring holes into her flesh and under her skin. Kat couldn't stop the blush that heated her cheeks.

"I wanted to have sex with you. The Trentians had nothing to do with that." He reached out his hand, willing her to take it. Kat looked at it and at him, her Cyborg, and went with her heart. She took it.

He pulled her to his side and held her close. His breath tickled the loose strands of her hair.

"I wanted you too," she whispered.

"I know. I could smell it."

"Oh. Gross."

He squeezed her hand. "A strong sense of smell helps when I hunt."

Kat sniffed him too, discerning nothing, not even the natural smell of a human. Dommik didn't have an organic smell and it unnerved her. *He really is...something else.* She laid her head against his chest. "Can I ask you something?"

"Depends."

"What happened that made the EPED force you to take on an employee?"

140

He didn't respond, not immediately, and she could have sworn she felt the metal frame of him shift under his skin where she touched him. It was almost like he was tensing up, but not quite. Muscles didn't physically shift to the side. Kat remained still and waited, for him to speak and for his interior shell to move.

"I was sent to a barely habitable planet, far off the main spaceways. It was called Argo." Dommik paused and that eerie feeling of foreboding came back to her.

"I've never heard of a planet called Argo."

"Argo-566 to be exact. It was a dust ball, another one of the billion lifeless planets on our maps charted out long ago by some of our first navigational and mapping scientists before I was created, and long before the great alien war."

"Oh."

"Several years ago, reports surfaced and pictures were uploaded by another Cyborg onto the Network of life on that planet, not just microscopic life, but plants and, well, creatures. The EPED got ahold of the images. They became interested and wanted to know more." He spun one of her curls. "I was sent there about a year ago to verify, scope out, and prove one way or another that it was habitable and that it could sustain a military base or at best a port. It's a standard job, not one we receive often, but not unusual."

"We?"

"Other Cyborgs that work for the EPED. You met two, Gunner and Netto."

Kat settled closer into Dommik, getting comfortable despite her aches, and watched the universe fly by. "I didn't realize there were others like you. Do they all have a double set of arms?"

"Some have other...well, let's call them parts, but we're all different." He continued, "It took several weeks before I arrived at the planet, and I found something very unusual. Planetary perimeter blockades, satellites, and relays. Someone was there, or at least was watching and guarding the place. I assumed outlaws. Tech isn't my specialty, but I was able to override it and hide my presence. I should've known then, that something was off, and I did for the most part, but I chose not to regroup and turn back. So I landed, or I tried to." Dommik stopped.

She draped her leg over his outstretched one and fingered the buckles of his chest piece with her free hand. Kat didn't know how she knew, but this story was harder for him than she anticipated and tried to comfort him the best way she could. "Why couldn't you land?"

"Because I couldn't see it."

Kat looked up at him. "How is that possible?"

"It was covered in corpses."

Chapter Thirteen:

. . . .

"**W**hat?" Kat lifted away and looked at him with shock.

Dommik could count the number of times he had ever been disturbed, and that count didn't go past his first hand. But that day did something to him that he couldn't fully understand: it had changed him, evolved him beyond the physical restraints of his body. There were new parts, software and hardware updates, there was even new technology, like his body-suit, that upgraded him. They didn't prepare him for Argo. And they didn't prepare him for Kat.

He didn't know why he felt compelled to tell her about it.

"There was no ground to be seen because it was covered up. And even within my ship, I could smell the stench, it was everywhere and it clung to everything. I was expecting a desert. Eventually, after several hours of flying over the dead, I gave up and landed amongst the waste. The ship popped the bloated things it landed on and settled into. After my vessel scanned the vicinity, it managed to find life amongst the dead, at least what remained and it was deep, and I mean *deep* underground.

I geared up and went out to investigate. It took some time, but I managed to dig my way to the planet's surface only to discover that the dead things had lived beneath the sands and the creatures on my radar were likely the same as the ones on the surface. I don't know what happened, but it drove the beasts from underground to die planetside." Dommik reached for Kat again and brought her back against him.

"What did you do?" she asked.

"My job. I found a tunnel and went after the live ones."

"How does this involve you needing me? You made it back."

"I did." Dommik sighed. "But it wasn't that simple. I went down into the tunnel and the live ones began to move toward the surface. They started to move toward me as well and I was ready for it. I thought it was a lucky break on my part and managed to catch several of the small ones, young I assumed at the time; and as I was retreating back to my ship with the paralyzed beasts dragging behind me, the tunnel collapsed."

"Oh my God."

Dommik laughed. "Maybe. Maybe not." He sobered up. "I was alive, partially crushed, for nearly a week and for a good portion of that time I was unconscious. I'm not sure how much you know about Cyborgs, but we heal at an extremely fast rate and we can survive without food and water for months before our nanocells begin to fail. My body was healing itself around crushed metal and I couldn't breathe, I couldn't estimate my time of death, and I so very much wanted to die. On the fifth day, I turned myself off and waited for it to happen."

"Why did you wait so long?"

"I was hoping one of the beasts would open up a tunnel nearby or through me and the ones I had captured would perish long before they woke up."

"So how did you get out?" He felt her body shiver against him.

"Remember those satellites and perimeter blockades I mentioned? Well, my override didn't work and alerted the owner. It was the Cyborg who first uploaded the images of life out there to the network. He had come to dispose of me, of my ship, but ended up saving me instead. He tracked my signal down and we connected wirelessly. It took him two days to get me out. In exchange for letting me live and healing me, I had to keep the EPED from getting involved. I docked my ship to his and we left Argo together."

Kat moved onto his lap and started kissing his jaw, light touches, just the barest hint of her lips that were dry but still soft and velvet. The parts inside him that wanted to shift into his *other* form became harder for him to keep under control. Dommik settled with letting her do what she wanted.

He continued, "I was out of commission for months and had my humanity off even longer. We stayed out in the fringes during that time so my ship couldn't be tracked. I was off the grid, completely, for an entire season. And when my reports were filed through, they had already assumed my death."

She stopped kissing and looked at him. "Why would they assume that? Did they even send someone out there to find you?"

"They didn't, couldn't, each mission costs them a significant amount of money and is queued far in advance. Even if they jumped my rescue to the top of the list, it would have taken them months to get there, at best. I have the best track record of any hunter in keeping communication with the EPED, so when I vanished they assumed the worst. Gunner of all Cyborgs was the only one who fought to go look for me. Keep kissing me," he demanded, harsher than he intended.

She looked away from him, "Okay," and leaned in, her mouth as light and airy as a butterfly. He flexed and grabbed her legs, pulling her firmly into his lap to straddle and sit on his hard-on.

"I know you want me."

"Well, Cyborg, I know you want me too. Finish the story. What happened when you returned?"

"Shock, confusion for the most part and quite a bit of anger. I told them the planet was dead and couldn't sustain life, that I had taken an injury and had recovered, and I would not tell them more. In return, they withheld payment for the mission and business went on as usual. They didn't believe me, of course, but they couldn't afford to lose me either. In retaliation, they have kept me on the easiest jobs since and close to Earth. And here you are, and here we are on my first mission since Argo, heading to a place they are probably hoping will get rid of you so they can put one of their own on this ship."

Kat shook her head and stopped feathering kisses on him again. "I don't understand," she leaned back to find his eyes. "Why did you have to keep Argo a secret? Why does a dead planet matter so much? Did he...did the other Cyborg kill it?"

"He told me there was a disease there, something he came into contact with and he took it upon himself to keep it contained."

"And you believed him?"

"Yes and even if I didn't. I owed him a life debt. I owe him a lot more. He fixed me, metal frame and all. I can't even begin to tell you how much money that would have cost him. All he asked for was silence and so I paid up."

She looked at him, head canted and questioning with messy hair framing her heart-shaped face and lips pressed firm into a straight line. Dommik lost control when she parted her lips to speak. "No more questions," he mumbled and kissed her. She swallowed her words with a moan and kissed him back.

He took her lips with a desperation he didn't know was inside him, a need for her exotic, unknowable taste in his mouth, simmering and wild. She parted her velvet soft mouth under his and gave him access to take her as burning, chaotic desire lit up between them. A wildfire, explosive and uncontrollable. Dommik needed her like this, always like this, and only ever for him.

Kat's hands gripped his shirt and tore it as she dragged her hands down his chest, his abs, over his pelvis and found the cock she was currently sitting on. He didn't stop her when she began to dance on him, rubbing him through his body-suit, with her fingers and her pussy.

Dommik grabbed her ass and thrust her against him. She gasped as he leveraged her above him and pulled down her pants, only letting her stand to rip them off all while she tore at his buckles, freeing him.

His dick sprang up, hard and thick, lusting to be sheathed by her, his little dripping-wet spitfire. With the light of the stars at her back, he could see her drenched panties and the sparkle of her essence at the crux of her thighs.

"I want to see you," he groaned, trying to control the uncontrollable.

Dommik kept his hands on her skin, caressing her legs as she stood up and shimmied out of her underwear. He kicked them up with his boot and pocketed them. Her knees came down to straddle him again.

And with her pussy just above him, in line to be impaled by him, his little fairy opened herself before his gaze and up on display. One hand on his shoulder for support, the other spreading her folds as she leaned slightly back. "Do you like it?"

He had been with several women in his life, all bought under mutual agreement, all when he was first created and he couldn't say anything about them, only faceless transactions, shadows in the dark and a minor reprieve to all the bloodshed and death. But Kat was different, alive, and blooming with supple curves, piercing eyes, and hair that was the embodiment of feral. Something that he didn't know that he so desperately needed.

He was going to keep her. Dommik knew from the moment she walked onto his ship and amongst his cages, he was going to keep her.

"You're beautiful." His fingers replaced hers. "I'm going to play with you. You might want to hold on."

She reached down and grabbed his cock, making him shudder. "I'm going to play with you too, then." She began to massage his long length.

Dommik tensed, his legs strained as delicate, exploratory hands coaxed him from his thick mushroom tip to his base and lower to explore his balls. Beads of his precum sprouted from him to trail down his girth and catch over her delicate fingers.

He looked away and focused on her rosy clit, a delicious beacon, that made his girl jerk with each flick and pinch of his fingers, every twitch bringing her wet opening closer to his cock. His thumb rubbed her bud with slow, measured movements as the rest of his hands explored her slick folds and stroked her everywhere, everywhere but her entrance, rounding it over and over, working her into a frenzy.

"Do you ache?" he groaned.

"Yes, but I don't care!" she had stopped kneading his cock, and only gripped him now, lost in her own hell. "I feel so empty." Kat tugged at him.

Dommik pierced her with his middle finger. "Is that better?" His thumb continued to rub her clit as he cupped her sex. She let go of him and grabbed his head, tearing at his hair and found his mouth to answer him with a fevered kiss.

"No," Kat hissed into him.

He found her puckered G-spot and brought her to climax with a stream all over his hand. It was wet and glorious.

"How about now?" he teased as she writhed and rode out each spasm, crying out each time he pressed her tender flesh. She rode his hand like how he was about to make her ride his straining Cyborg cock.

When her second orgasm hit, clenching his lone finger, he let go and thrust her down on his waiting erection, taking every swollen inch she had to give. Dommik held her as her body pumped his. With only her moans spearing him on, he took her hips and moved her. He took in her every quiver, her every heartbeat, and kissed every inch of skin his mouth could reach.

He worshiped her as she succumbed to him.

And when her tired hands slowly lifted her shirt above her head to reveal her flushed breasts and perky nipples, he filled her with his seed. Kat's thighs slapped his mid thrust. He held her over him until all of his seed was spent deep within her pussy. Until her deliciously pink sex strangled his cock and sucked every drop out of him.

Dommik was ready for round two, but the urgency and the chaos ebbed into sated exhaustion. He took it for what it was and caressed her back as he held her. "You make me feel alive," he whispered after a while.

She made his heart bleed.

"You just make me tired."

Dommik laughed. "That's all? No 'I'm the best you've ever had?' That I make you feel alive too? Give a man something to work with."

He heard Kat scoff and snort. "Fine. You make my muscles ache too."

"I can help with that." He kissed the top of her head and pulled her off his lap, off his cock, buckling himself and picking her up. She mumbled protests but didn't try to move away.

"Where are we going?"

"Medbay."

She tensed in his arms.

What are you hiding from me?

He had told her one of his secrets; it was now time for Kat to tell him one of hers.

Chapter Fourteen:

• • • •

"**I** don't need to go to medbay, I was teasing about the aches. They're so minor I'll be better after a night's rest," Kat teased...and pleaded.

"And what about your cramps?"

"The beginning of a monthly. Can't you tell?" She blushed and squinted when they entered the bay and the bright white lights powered on. It was always a shock to be in a well-lit room these days. It was even more so to see the Cyborg without his cloak of shadows. "Look, I should go check my message log and get back to Mia. Shouldn't you be piloting?" *Please work.*

He set her gently on a pallet. "Are you afraid? A nurse, afraid of being looked at?"

"I saw Dr. Cagley yesterday, I'm fine," she said as the pain of her cramps came back, making her flinch.

Kat sat up and watched as Dommik grabbed a reader off the wall and came towards her. *What if he finds something? I don't want him to know my medical history.* Kat went to stand when his arm snaked around her waist and pressed her back onto the bed.

"I know you're hiding something from me, Kat. I know when I'm being lied to by humans." He warned, but released her. She didn't breathe. "But I won't force you to tell me."

He lifted the medical reader between them, expectantly, waiting for her to come clean. She bit the inside of her cheek and glared at him in challenge. *Damn you.* "Was Argo a lie?"

Dommik looked surprised at the question and she felt a twinge of guilt.

"No."

"Then why are you trying to get to know me? You could barely stand me not even yesterday morning." Kat tugged the sheet from under her and wrapped it around her naked body. She couldn't help but flinch as he set down the reader with rage furrowing his brows.

He made her angry by being angry.

"What's it going to be? I let you back on my ship, I opened myself up to you and not because of forming some sort of connection between us, but because you chose this course. You chose me and whether you thought about it or not, you chose to go with me into Trentian airspace." He leaned over her, making her fall back into the bed. "You trust me with your life, but you won't trust me with your secrets?"

Kat glared at him while her heart raced in tempo with the medical equipment's light. She glanced at the reader sitting next to her and decided.

There's nothing wrong with me. He won't find anything. And if he does...

It wouldn't matter anyway.

She picked up the instrument and handed it to him. He took it from her slowly, their fingers brushed against each other sending electric shivers through her.

"You won't find anything," she whispered and laid back. Their eyes remained locked as he flipped on the machine and ran it over her body.

"Then what are you so worried about?" he asked, his anger tempered.

"I don't know."

His eyes left hers as he ran each of her limbs under the reader, quietly, tenderly and almost as if he was polite about it, if he sneaked up on it, there wouldn't be anything to find. *Like a hunter.* Kat steadied herself.

One arm down. Her hand. Her fingers. The other arm, up from her palm and over her shoulder and neck.

Nothing.

The readings were beyond her sight, but she watched Dommik's face. It was all she needed to know.

He ran it over her chest, her torso and each breast. Kat's breathing picked up. Down he went over her ribs, running his knuckles over her after each swipe of the reader. Until it reached her stomach and his movements went even slower, eyes hooded and concentrating.

His face cringed. His finger tapped.

It beeped.

Her heart exploded from her chest and his hand clamped down on her shoulder and pinned her to the table.

Kat's eyes flooded with tears while her body struggled for freedom.

"Calm down!" He set the reader out of her reach.

154

"What's wrong with me?" she cried. "I don't want to die." Kat stared at the machine just out of her reach and continued to fight for it, fight him.

"You're not dying." Dommik pulled her into his chest and held her tight. "Why do you think you're dying?" Kat fought until her breath gave up...until her muscles melted and ached. He didn't let go nor did his hold on her lessen. She was jailed. It warmed her body but not her mind.

"What did the machine say?" she settled into him, out of breath. He picked her back up and left the bay behind. Her eyes didn't leave the reader until it was out of sight.

He laughed under his breath, "Pretty much that you've had vigorous sex recently." Kat looked up and they were back in the star alcove, their clothes now folded on the seat beside them.

"My grandmother died."

Dommik caught her chin and forced her to look at him. His lips downcast.

Emotion looks odd on a Cyborg. "I'm sorry," he said.

"We were close. Very close." Kat stared at the wall, remembering. "We went through a lot together, two people who had no one else in the universe, separated by generations and entirely different experiences but that couldn't change how we felt. She died a month before you and I met."

"Is she why you're afraid to die?" He combed his fingers through her hair, but it didn't comfort her.

Kat let out a crazed laugh. "I help people die. I know death. I hold their hands until they breathe their last breath and death takes them away from me. I was born into the profession." She shifted in his embrace. "Like how you were created for yours."

He didn't say anything.

"I'm afraid to die...because I think I will." Kat let it out and closed her eyes.

"Don't talk about something unless you want that something to happen. The devil hears everything."

"Did you kill someone?"

She jerked. *What?* "No, I've never killed anyone."

"I've killed many."

"How many?"

"I've pumped people full of so much poison they never wake up, I've torn out their throats with my teeth, sliced them into a thousand pieces with my claws, and shot countless more. I've looked Death in the eye and have been him myself. It's a raw look, Kat, his eyes. They don't look back at you but through you, into you, until you're no longer breathing, no longer thinking. Then he disappears and leaves you cold and you hate and fear him all the more for it. You might know it, but what you do, helping people die, is far closer to heaven than it is to hell."

Kat found herself holding him tighter in a comforting embrace that matched his own. "I'm sorry, Cyborg." She kissed his chest.

"Don't be. The difference between you and me, angel, is that I love what I do."

She shook her head, "That's not true. I love what I do too. It haunts me because it feels right, but it makes me a hypocrite because I don't want to die. I'm afraid of dying."

Dommik held her close as she told him her story, the way she had been born and never held by her mother, watching her parents die miserably behind a glass barrier, being in quarantine for the first third of her life, up to her choice in letting her grandmother die on her own terms. Leaving Kat to pick up the pieces and clean up the fallout.

She told him about the Gliese parasite and how she lived each day that she might have it hidden within her.

It was word vomit. Her neuroses on display for him to digest and judge at his own free-will, and she hated being judged. Kat had stopped telling her story when she was barely out of her pre-teen years because of how people reacted. Pity and fear. Pity for the domesticated medical animal she was and fear that she could be a host to a creature that would destroy them from the inside out.

When she was finished, Kat didn't feel better. Her heart felt as heavy as it always had and she knew that whatever Dommik would decide, life would go on and her burdens would remain.

They sat in silence. Not by choice but because he had yet to respond to her past. Kat waited with every frozen fiber of her being.

"Were you," she watched as Dommik tried to find his words, "were you a virgin when I claimed you?" It was the first time she saw real emotion in his eyes.

Kat blushed. "No. I wouldn't have potentially killed someone, but I was not a virgin."

"Who was he?" His question came out harsh, edged with venom.

"It's not what you think," She stammered and had to look away embarrassed. "One of my patients, doomed to die from a genetic disorder. We became close and he knew what could be in me, but it didn't matter to him. He was going to die anyway. I held his hand also."

"I'm sorry."

His apology embarrassed her more.

"It's in the past." She leaned up and kissed his lips. "I like knowing I can't hurt you. That you're safe to touch, to kiss. I would say it's my favorite thing about you, but it's not." Kat said into his chest.

"What is your favorite thing about me? You have me curious."

"Right now? My favorite thing is that you're not disgusted by me." Her courage grew. "You're so..."

"Monstrous?"

"No. Thoughtful, you're thoughtful. I like that the most."

He kissed the top of her head and she felt the familiar intake of his breath, consuming her. "You're not sick, Kat. You need to listen to me. There is nothing inside you. And today I don't want you to think of it again, ever again. Do you hear me? You're not near death anymore. You're an assistant to a monster hunter and what we do prevents death."

"Okay." Kat swallowed. "I'll try." She lied.

"I need to show you something."

She let out a stale breath and got up when he moved to stand. She pulled on her clothes while he watched. Dommik took her hand in his and led her back to the menagerie. The half empty room that was encased in heavy layers of steel and reinforced glass cages. The androids were milling about keeping the creatures within healthy and hopefully...happy.

He led her to the one room she hated the most. The roaches.

Always the bugs.

The door closed behind them, and the bright light blinded her. They stood in front of her least favorite case. He let go of her hand and opened it up.

Kat jumped back as he pried the roaches off of a branch that she had fed them earlier. They critters scattered away from him, some up his arms, over the interior of the glass. She was on the other side of the room while Dommik picked the bugs off of himself and enclosed them again. Kat was gagging by the end.

"Why would you do that?" she coughed with disgust. Shaking herself as if they had crawled all over her instead. "Now I'm really going to be sick."

A mangled and chewed on plant appeared in front of her face. "Take it," Dommik demanded of her.

She gripped it with the edge of her two fingers and held it away. "Why?"

"That's the plant that you think killed your parents. Nargeo."

Kat flung it away from her in horror.

In shock.

"It's harmless," he said.

But she didn't hear him.

The ship's speakers went on and transmitted the one message that saved her from herself:

"*Warning. Warning. Entering Trentian territory.*"

159

Chapter Fifteen:

• • • •

Dommik sat in the bridge, alone, his eyes and half his systems monitoring the channels and spaceways around his ship. With each day, each hour that went by, heading deeper into alien territory, hey moved closer to Xan'Mara and to the solar system that heralded the Trentian homeworld, Xanteaus Trent.

They hadn't run into any scout ships yet, but that didn't mean anything. He sensed in his mechanical gut that the aliens knew he had crossed their borders. They may not have been as technologically advanced as the Earthians, but they had their ways...unexplainable ways.

The Space Lords and Knights that protected the Trentian species had abilities that couldn't be explained scientifically. The thousands of autopsies the Earthians performed on the dead showed nothing of their powers. *No tech in their bodies.*

It was either that or they had a better way of hiding it than his creators.

Peace treaties my ass.

He wasn't afraid of the aliens: he was created for the purpose of hunting them down and killing them. That programming could never be changed. And it was always the bottom line deep inside, ready and waiting for the day when he needed to revert back to his basic self. Until then, he was a monster hunter for the EPED.

He was also soon to be a father.

Dommik scraped his hand down his face. Kat had no idea he released his nanocells, preprogrammed to impregnate her, deep within her womb. Cyborgs couldn't have children, but here he was, breaking the cybernetic law and jeopardizing his brethren's hard-won peace.

There was only one way to truly claim a mate in the eyes of a Trentian, and that was a child. If she was forced to encounter any of them while in their territory, they'd not only smell him all over her skin–which should be enough to satisfy them–but also be able to sense the baby growing within her.

My baby. He slammed his fist into the console, crushing a series of buttons. It sparked and crackled, lighting up the area around it in a glow. Dommik placed his hand on top of the flare and let himself burn as the room faded back into darkness. He watched as the outline of his hand brightened into an orange halo and the smell of burnt flesh filled the room.

He wasn't infallible and he would be the first one to say he wasn't experienced at wooing a girl. This one he desperately wanted and that desperation marred his common sense.

Dommik clicked on the security feed and found Kat's heat signature in her quarters, barricading herself within the only place she thought was her own, holing up away from him.

It had been days since he handed her the half-eaten plant, days since her eyes widened in shock and the weed hit the floor. He thought facing her fear would help her recover from her trauma, but now he understood something else...

You can't heal a human with the switch of a button.

Humans didn't have internal technology to cure them. They didn't have a switch to turn themselves off.

He tried to comprehend what it was like to be fully human, to not have the security of metal and steel lining his organs, to not have another program to update his systems. He tried to imagine what it was like to be vulnerable, unable to improve one's existence, unable to regulate one's hormones. To fall victim to your body's chemistry.

Dommik couldn't imagine it. Even compared to other Cyborgs, he was less human, less humane and he had to fake it. Sometimes he was even successful.

All he could imagine was *her.*

Her pixie features and flushed body. Her moans as he sank deep inside of her, mewing like a kitten or the curls that wanted to spring out of his grip and resume their freedom. Her nipples bouncing with each of his thrusts as he forced her tight pussy to take him, all of him. Over and over until her eyes hooded with exhaustion.

He saw her struggling, trapped within his web of ropes, with drips of arousal gliding down her inner thighs, bound, waiting, and needy, begging him for everything.

Dommik let his animal instincts take over his head, succumbing to the fantasies he so desperately wanted to make real. His unburned hand wrapped around the steel length of his cock while his other fried. His cum shot out onto the floor into a white puddle of unused seed.

Seed that should be in her.

"Fuck!" Dommik lifted his hand from the circuitry and watched his skin heal. He listened as the ventilation cleared the smell of his wound from the bridge.

He yanked out a tool kit from his back port and got to work fixing the machine, wishing he knew what to do about his fairy.

• • • •

A CHIME ON HER DOOR woke her up.

"Go away," Kat yelled out, curling up tight into a fetal position, succumbing to the nausea that was trying to drown her. She smacked her lips and swallowed the sour taste of her breath.

The door whipped open. She balled up further under her thin blanket.

"Please go away," she mumbled this time.

Her only covering tore away as familiar hands, four of them, lifted her off the bed and into a cradle of arms. She knew Dommik had four arms, but the initial shock of feeling all of them at once made her shriek.

"You can't stay in here all day, every day. Face the fucking light, Kat." Dommik set her on her bare feet.

She slapped at his chest. "What light!? What light? The only light on this ship is in the one place I don't want to go! Unless you mean the alcove but that's off limits to me," she yelled again. "I hate you."

163

Dommik hauled her like a petulant child to the lavatory. She dragged her feet. *If you want obnoxious, I'll give you obnoxious!*

But her nausea swallowed her up, causing her struggles to falter as she dry heaved. She felt the tug of her hair, held away from her face, and his arms rubbing her back as she coughed and gagged. When her fit eased and nothing but spittle was left on her bottom lip, Dommik walked her to the shower. Kat hunkered onto the metal floor away from the spray of water as it warmed up.

He stripped and got into the stall with her. "I hate you," she said again.

"I know." He sat down with her, naked. "I wish I could say I was sorry, but I'm not. Talk to me."

The water sprayed off him and landed on her, drenching her nightshirt. "How could you even have that horrible thing on your ship? Why make me hold it?"

"Because it's harmless. The parasite was eradicated years ago, it can't hurt you, it can do nothing to you unless you let it." One of his hands brushed up against her lips, wiping her clean. Kat jerked forward and bit his finger. "Did that make you feel better?" He didn't move his hand.

She let him go. "I wish it did."

"Would keeping the plant a secret from you have made you happier?"

Kat held back her tears. "No."

"Do you wish you had stayed in Ghost, far away from me, away from the secrets we shared?" Dommik's voice grew harder with each question.

"No."

"Do you regret opening up to me?"

Tears formed on her eyelids. "I don't know." She bent her knees up to her chest and watched as he grabbed something from outside the stall. He handed her a disk of medication.

"What's this?"

"Something that will relieve your nausea and help with your cramps. Synthesized Ano Algae from Elyria. Take two a day. You're suffering from a vitamin D deficiency as well, common for first-time space travelers. It will help."

"Thank you," she whispered and took it from him, gripping it close.

"Do you want to know a secret?"

Kat rubbed her eyes and was about to say no again but stopped her robotic response. "Yes," she whispered into the water.

"You're an angel." Warm, wet hands cupped her cheeks as he forced her to look at him. "An angel. You have to move on. You have a–"

Incoming sirens blared.

Dommik looked up and away from her, his sentence unfinished at the tip of his tongue. One of the Bins walked into the lavatory as he stood up, tense and straight. Kat felt cold under the hot water.

"What's wrong? What's happening?" His muscles bulged and his jaw broke off his face before reattaching. "Dommik?"

The siren rang once again. "It's a hail. We have company." He turned toward her, long hair against his white skin appearing like trails of oil on water. "Go to your room and get dressed."

165

Kat climbed up to her knees. "What were you going to say before?"

His eyes flew over her body, prickled and glistening. Her body priming itself for his dominion. He could have taken her from behind, forced her to call him master, and she would have let him.

The moment passed.

"Stay quiet. They can't take you away from me."

Chapter Sixteen:

• • • •

He didn't need to answer the call to know they had company. Dommik just needed to look outside the bridge's window to see the giant white ship. It looked like a droplet of rain, a thin yet curved bullet that peaked at the end into a series of needles where the thrusters and warp drives were stored. It had a smoky quality to it, a very alien look. The sides jutted out like a serrated knife, a puffer fish's spikes just waiting to spear an unassuming vessel in its wake.

He knew those spikes. He knew they were made with Pryzian metal and what that metal could do. He had it inside him. It could puncture the soul from a being, or the lifeblood of nearby flyer. The spikes ejected outward like a spring and stabbed everything they came in contact with. Only to retreat and do it again.

Only one type of Trentian captained a *Piercer Battleship*. A Space Lord hailed him.

Dommik sighed and sat down, answering the chime.

"This is the *Spider* answering, Captained by Dommik, myself, a Cyborg in service to the Earthian Planetary Exploration Division. We have business to take care of within the Trentian sectors."

"Dommik," an alien hissed low through the channel. "Dommik. Why do you have hundreds of lifeforms on our radar, inside your ship, if you only have business here? Dommik." It slithered strong and hateful through his speaker system. A hidden curse to his name.

Names were important to the aliens, just like women, and flesh. He knew what he was dealing with, but Kat would be nothing but gold to a dragon.

"I apologize. Who am I speaking to?"

Laughter, merciless laughter answered. Dommik counted the guns he had within reach arm's reach in his head.

"A Space Lord, Cyborg, a Lord to your created existence, bright within Xanteaus's eyes. But if you must, must know a name to continue this intrigue, it is thus: Markoss, Lord of Light's Reach. Answer me NOW," his voice went from a hissing whisper to a bomb readying to ignite.

"I have cargo, recovered for the EPED, creatures from other worlds to study and plants to examine. All in the name of expansion and safety for both our peoples and the hybrids we create," Dommik leaned back, hoping he had a fiber of charm in his body.

Charm, hah.

"Cyborgs don't create life, Dommik. They take it. Where has your council sent you and what for?"

"The mission is classified," he rolled his eyes to the ceiling.

"Can you classify death?"

"Of course."

"Shall I speak the ritual of the unhonored before we immobilize you and take you in?"

"Do you really, really want to fire on a Cyborg, Space Lord? Because that wouldn't go well for you. Even if you take down my ship, it won't hurt me. I'll survive out in space and cling to you like a shadow, weigh you down with overrides and webs until you go crazy with trying to get rid of a bug that Just Won't Die."

"Ah, there are the threats I am used to from your kind, so much bark, so much bite!" he chuckled with glee. "I am not trying to start a war. I am offering death. Unless you would take another route with me? How about an inspection and allowance to move on through my jurisdiction? What brings you to our space anyway, wired-being?"

Dommik answered this time. "I've been sent by the EPED to procure an O'lia flower to catalog its...mythical capabilities. Xan'Mara is my destination."

"Is that so? I can tell you all about the flower right now, Cyborg," the alien said with a taunt.

"I'm afraid that's not good enough, Alien. Our scientists want one on hand."

"That flower. That flower will not live within captivity, it will not follow your orders, it will never survive a trip to..." the alien spat it out, "Earth."

Dommik sat back and leaned his heavy frame into the back of his chair. *What if I procure the flower and it's dead on delivery? I'll bring the seeds.*

"That's not a problem for me."

The Space Lord silenced the line with a static fizzle.

"You can take one."

"One flower?"

"No seeds."

"And what If I don't agree? What if I go to Xan'Mara and ask the pilgrims for an orchard? Take a handful of seeds? Will you engage in a space battle with a Cyborg?"

A huffing breath filled his ears. "One flower. One, Dommik, and an inspection of your ship. We can't allow unknown life into our system."

"No."

"No? That's not good enough, Dommik. You have limited options, Dommik. Dommik. You can allow my eyes through your passageways or you can blow up into dust. You Cyborgs are said to possess reason. Life or death?"

"You mean life or a Cyborg parasite?"

Dommik could feel the shrug the Space Lord twitched through the intercom. He blew on his healing hand, letting his uncertain breath out of his system. *What does it matter? Kat is mine. Mine. Mine.* He repeated the words in his head.

"Fine, you can inspect my ship, but only you. We will put our faces in each other's eyes and measure, and you will find truth in mine. Let's waste some time, as you seem to be dead-set on the idea." He allowed his ship to connect with the aliens. Every bump and grind of the tunnel that shot out and connected their ships scraped at the back of his eyes.

Several lifeforms waited for him on the other side and Dommik went to meet them at the docking bay, well away from the hull and Kat. He stripped himself of all his weapons, several knives, a gun, and darts slick with his own poison.

It didn't make him any less scary, any less threatening, but if he knew one thing about the aliens he was designed to kill, he knew ritual was important to them and one didn't bring weapons to a peaceful meeting. He waited while the docking completed, staring at the metal wall that separated him from his old enemy.

Dommik made a fist then quickly shook out his violence. He locked it down, tight, and the door swished open to three beings even paler than he was but with pearlescent veins of different colors.

The Space Lord stood in front, a bipedal humanoid that had his white hair cut close to his head, a plain helmet, forest green, hung at his hip. A scythe made of diamond was strapped to his back, and even in the low light of the tunnel, it was too brilliant to look at. A trickster weapon. Only the Lord Markoss carried; his lackeys with long, braided hair were unarmed.

They carried, breaking the ritual. Dommik was a weapon in his own right.

Each Trentian wore gloves. Dommik made sure of it, eyeing their hands, uncaring that they knew he looked. Lord Markoss lifted his wrists to show him the buckles that secured his gauntlets in place.

He nodded, "Let's get this over with." The aliens followed him into his ship.

"If only we could trust each other, Cyborg, we would create the greatest army." Rainbows shot out and danced with each footstep, created by the diamond blade.

"If only we could trust each other."

Markoss laughed softly.

Dommik led them to the central interior where the EPED had stamped their name and symbol into the walls and floors. A lonely place that he never visited. "Now you have your proof and it's even written on

171

the walls for you. No battle. One flower. And we can leave here honoring our people's peace agreement."

The alien lord walking around the exterior circuit of the room, watching his steps and reading his ship's history. It twinkled in his green eyes. Like Kat's but silent and eerie. They wanted to kill each other. The tension was obvious and deadly.

"Dommik. Dommik. Dommik, where are the beings on board this ship? You must have a crew you are hiding away..."

He clenched his hand again. "Come," he canted his head. "I'll show you, for two flowers and safe passage." When the alien chuckled again and trailed behind him, the terms were agreed.

They rode down the elevator in silence, facing each other, muscles ticking, sizing the other up. "Why do you want the O'lias?"

"I don't. The people I work for do. Why do you wear your hair short?"

"Ah, so you noticed," Markoss mocked. "Not every Trentian plays by the rules. Which could only mean one thing..."

"You broke the law."

"I hate wearing my hair long. It's bothersome. I cut it off." The doors opened.

Dommik could smell Kat, her scent lingering in the air. The ventilation systems had not yet filtered her out. The aliens showed no sign that they knew she was there. Dommik kept his mind on his enemies as he led them to the facility, and they stopped short when his glass enclosures came into view.

The androids continued their work as if nothing unusual was happening. They swept her presence away, benignly working on the tech. Immobilized under his control. Bin-Three stood sentinel down the hallway, around the darkened corner. One of his Bins started up the ventilation.

"The androids are my crew, they do my bidding. You won't find another being except for the creatures, so count them if you must." He walked to the roach room and opened the door. "It might take you awhile."

Markoss peered in and out, several seconds at most. "Three hundred and eighty-three. There are two creatures in that glass tower and four more in that one." The alien indicated the Drogluks, a birdlike creature that can fly in multiple atmospheres with ease, wanted for study in durability. "There is a handful of walled off plants over there. I see no bugs outside the enclosures. It doesn't quite add up." Markoss turned to look at him. "Are you a liar, Cyborg?"

"No." Dommik lied without a beat. "There are no other lifeforms on this ship." He imagined Kat, sitting quietly in her quarters.

"I want to believe you, but I just can't. We will accompany you to Xan'Mara and inspect your ship upon retrieval of the flowers. Unless you show me what you are hiding."

Dommik breathed, letting his body fill with sterilized air. He kept his mind on Kat while he let the code deep inside him that told him to kill all Trentians fall back into its shallow grave.

"Let me see you off," he gritted his teeth. "One O'lia it is." The metal plates in his jaw tightening, each step a test of his willpower to not tear the aliens apart. The four of them didn't make a sound, gliding as trained predators would out of the menagerie; when the barely audible coughing, a strangled moan, followed by a sharp intake of breath for a lost silence came through the multi-layered steel barriers, it was as loud as thunder. And just as damning.

Markoss pulled his scythe out, slow and lazy, a sway of power and hooked it around his neck. Dommik relaxed as it pressed into his skin as the smell of copper filled the air.

"I don't like liars, Dommik."

Dommik shifted. His extra limbs pulled away from his metal frame, his fingers and toes locking into eight sharp claws all while only losing a single drop of blood. He speared the aliens lord's lackey's into the ground. "Make a wrong move, Markoss, and your friends are dead."

"Not before you lose your head. Is it a girl?" They stood their ground, each a cut away from death.

"She's mine."

"She sounds sick. Show her to me and I will be the judge of that."

"I could kill you a thousand different ways, Alien. Diamond can't cut through my skeleton. Not before your death."

"Dommik. Dommik. Dommik, try me. My blade has met your kind in battle."

"So have mine," he sneered, his bladed claws pressed deeper into the pinned down guards. They wouldn't move, wouldn't fight without their lord's command. "You're on my ship. You won't die honorably here. I'll make sure your bodies are never found."

"And you will not make it out of this sector without every Space Lord and Knight after you. Does this girl know you are a monstrosity? A disgusting eight-legged creature? Sometimes I wonder if there are redeeming qualities within the Earthians, but then something like you lands in my path."

Dommik didn't need to be told what he was, since he already knew. He didn't even look like a "spider" when he shifted, but more of a deformed *thing* with an arched back, stretched flesh, and exposed wiring. Many went into shock upon seeing his other form. He thought of Kat.

His limbs drew back into his body while his bio-suit reformed around his frame, his fingers breaking off from his claws, until he was a man again, a normal figure, with a pile of shredded clothes at his feet. The guards drew up and the scythe slipped from his neck, releasing him from its noose.

The cut had healed by the time Markoss settled his weapon back in place.

Dommik cracked his neck and calmed his heart. He didn't turn around to face his visitors.

She should have stayed in Ghost.

● ● ● ●

KAT TRIED TO STIFLE her cough, but it slipped through her fingers and into the waste basket she was bent over. Her stomach roiled and clawed at her insides. She broke the foil on her pill case and swallowed one. She gagged as it left a bitter taste in her mouth. Kat looked around. *I wish I had water.*

Her eyes landed on the door and stilled. She waited silently, trying in vain to discern any noises beyond but heard nothing, nothing but the sound of air flow. The pain in her gut ebbed. Her heartbeat rang like a bell to her ears, echoing like a roar throughout the small space as the familiar feeling of paranoia came back. Gingerly, Kat unzipped her pants and peered down into her panties.

No blood. She was either having the worst period of her life or something else was causing her pain.

Her ears pricked when she heard Dommik's familiar footsteps outside. The room was too small to rush the door, but she managed to get her clothes in order before it opened. She reached for him just as he took her into his arms, his face grim.

"What happened?" she asked as he led her into the hallway, undimmed now and startling. Her eyes caught the cascade of rainbows first, hundreds of colorful dots ran down the walls, blinding...and so very wrong for the interior of his ship.

The spider didn't have color. Unless it was the red glow that it bled out as light and pretend light was not the same as true color. Her life was black and white, just like Dommik.

That's when she saw the Trentians. Dommik gripped her arm, holding her close enough to know she'd have a new bruise within the hour.

"Hello, little one. What is your name?" The intimidating one with the weapon that blinded stepped forward. He spoke to her in a heavily accented Earthian. She looked up at her Cyborg expectantly, he nodded.

"Katalina. Kat for short," she narrowed her eyes. "If I like you."

The alien laughed. It didn't lighten the mood, and only made it worse. "Kat. Katalina. A catchall of a name, beautiful and robust, Lina and Katal and Talina for short. It is very Earthian, but I could see our women enjoying that namesake. Katalina."

Um.

"Thank you."

"Shall we talk privately?" he asked.

Dommik's hold on her tightened and it was then she noticed he was wearing only his bio-suit. "No," he answered for her.

"No?"

Kat pushed away. "Yes. We can talk privately." She had the full use of her mind now that her pain was gone. The alien bowed his head. Her curiosity wouldn't be denied.

Dommik pulled her close, his hand tangling in her hair. He whispered into her ear. "Don't let him touch you. If you need me, I'm a breath away. A heartbeat. A flinch and a whisper."

They were being scrutinized.

She twisted away. "You got into a fight. I can fix this," her hand waved at his attire. "I'm not an idiot and I don't plan on dying this day." She turned toward the Trentian. "We can speak in the hold. Have you seen it? There are some very interesting creatures we're traveling with."

The men let her through as she led them back to the enclosures. Dommik and the guards waited as she and the imposing leader left the group behind.

Kat wasn't going to impede this mission if she could help it. If she had to schmooze safe travel, she would. It's not like she wasn't already living in a highly un-gilded cage. The Trentians knew of her existence now. The androids milled about. Dommik could see through their eyes. It was safe.

"Dommik has shown us the creatures and has assured us that his hosts will not interrupt any of our ecosystems or be set free on any of our habitable planets."

Kat turned to the godly alien. He startled her like his rainbows, and if her heart hadn't already been taken away, she might've not been opposed to an abduction. She also wanted to hold his scythe.

"What's your name?" she asked, meeting his ethereal gaze.

"Space Lord, Markoss."

Her heart sank and she hugged herself away from him. "Lord Markoss," she bowed her head in the way he bowed his, "what do you want to talk about?"

"You and your captain have a way of getting to the point. Talina. Katalina."

"Yes." Kat was nervous but tried not to show it.

"Are you here by free-will?"

"Yes."

The alien clasped his hands behind his back.

"Has the Cyborg hurt you in any way?"

"No." *Damn him and his stupid roaches and plants.* She lied.

Markoss gifted her a chilling smile. "Are you claimed? I do not see a ring on your finger."

"Yes. Not by marriage."

"By Dommik?"

Kat sighed, "Yes." *Yes, yes, yes.*

"Your eyes are green." He walked around her and she shifted uncomfortably. "So are mine. It is a fine trait to have, Katalina." Markoss stopped again before her. "But I have no intention of taking claimed females even if they are claimed by liars. You see, Katalina, Cyborgs cannot have children which I can only assume..."

"I don't understand?"

"That you seek refuge."

Her confusion grew. "I'm not here for refuge," she said, unsure if she meant it as a question.

"Would you like to stay aboard this ship or would you like to seek refuge on mine?" The Space Lord reached his hand out, offering it up to be taken. Or left cold and undisturbed.

Fine ghostly fingers cupped into a shallow half-circle before her, with beautiful braids of green veins that matched his eyes. Touching his hand would be life-altering and she wasn't sure why. Only that the creep of unease that prickled up her spine said so. Curiosity could kill the cat and despite her nerves, she found herself compelled to grasp it.

To be bound by it.

To be beloved and beholden to its grip, forever.

Her hand remained at her side.

"I choose to stay here." His hand disappeared in a blur back into his glove.

"Very well."

Kat half-staggered to the door. It zipped open to reveal Dommik's arms. Her confusion drifted away when he cocooned her in steel. She needed him, wanting him to know she chose him, and that, maybe, she would always choose him.

She had chosen him at the port, at Ghost, and now far into space, it was a revelation that sat unwell in her heart. *Would he choose me?* It hadn't mattered before.

They rode up the elevator together in silence, her arms banded around Dommik. He stopped them at the alcove. "Wait here," he let her go.

She wanted to bury her face into her hands and forget all about the aliens.

Markoss tilted his head in her direction. "It was nice to meet you, little one, Katalina, Katal, Lina, Talina. Congratulations. Kat?" They left her before she could respond and deny her abbreviated name. His voice remained in her head, snaking through and leaving only confusion in its wake.

She watched as they disappeared down the hallway until the rainbows faded into the dark.

Kat twirled her wristlet and mulled over her first interaction with an alien being. Earth had made it seem so very scary, and so unreal as if they were mythical, or an elaborate hoax played by the government to explain the significant amount of losses in deep space. It wasn't until the silence returned that she realized she was alone.

Kat looked around for Bin-Three and saw only empty shadows.

With the rush of adrenaline fueling her she darted into the forbidden part of the ship.

Chapter Seventeen:

. . . .

She wasn't quite sure where she was going, only that she had never been down these passageways before, had never been this deep into the ship. If someone had knocked her out and dropped her in one of the corridors blind, she would wake up thinking she was outside her quarters, that is, until the walls expanded twofold and the atmosphere became *commercial*.

A door popped open to her right, showing her the medbay. She peeked in to see the reader was still lying forgotten on the table. Kat made a note of it and continued.

The metal sheets, painted in pristine strips, glinted under the lowlights. The quality improved to make the crew's quarters look primitive in comparison. Perfect symmetry. Perfectly boring. She glanced back to find the way behind her looked like her way forward. *Don't get turned around.*

Dommik was going to find her, she was sure of it, but hopefully, she would find what he was hiding first. Over half the ship was off-limits and there could only be two reasons: he needed his space, or there was something he didn't want her to see.

A hand clamped down on her shoulder, pushing her into the wall. "What do you think you're doing?"

The cold wall seeped into her cheek. "Exploring. I wanted to see what you allowed the Trentians to see...but not me." Kat shivered. He spun her around to face him.

"I didn't bring them here," he hissed over her face. "You've caused me a lot of trouble and I'm wondering if you're worth it."

Kat pressed her hands into his chest. "You know everything about me, all my dark and terrible secrets. I've let you inside my body, I've let you cum all over my chest and you still hide away. I trust you, Dommik, and I shouldn't. I've wanted you the moment I saw you, but the Space Lord..."

"What about him?" he growled. "Choose your words well."

She looked away but he gripped her chin and tilted her head back. "He made me confused."

"That's all? Because that doesn't explain your trespassing." His frame blocked out the small amount of light.

"It was strange, almost compelling, and for a moment I really wanted to go with him. But then whatever juju he did vanished and I wanted to stay with you. He said some things," she swallowed, "he congratulated me and I have no idea *why*. I saw my opportunity to reassert myself and took it." Kat lifted her face. "I'm not sorry."

"I have rules for a reason and if I wanted you on the upper decks, I'd allow it. But I don't," he stormed. "I have not and I will not have you disobey my word." Kat winced as he took her arm and led her back to her jailed section and into the facility. He took the wristlet off her arm and crushed it in his fist. Bin-Three appeared at her side.

"I'm sorry," she whispered, hugging herself.

"You just said you weren't. False-fucking-bravado. Bin-Three will be at your side at all times. If you need to leave this room only it can allow you to do so." He turned away to leave her.

She surged forward to stop him. "Please, Dommik, I am sorry! I won't go up there again. I just..."

"Reflect on how badly you want to live, Katalina, because you have an idiotic tendency to play with your life." And then he was gone. "Even I can't save you from some things," his voice faded behind the door.

Kat looked around almost mystified that there weren't a thousand rainbows anymore. She glanced at the closed walls far and deep, the giant glass, to an empty zoo of enclosures and beyond to the few plants and animals, they were safeguarding. The closed door to the roaches, now beyond her reach, and the androids who ignored her, lifeless and yet observant.

She rested her gaze on Bin-Three.

Maybe she had made a mistake, maybe even a few of them, but she couldn't pinpoint one exact moment that changed her, considering there were a few of them.

But her mind wandered back to the upper decks. *What's up there?*

She hadn't seen anything off-putting, only the same series of doors over and over. If he was hiding something it was deeper in.

If the Trentians had seen something, it hadn't bothered them. Kat reached to grab the key-chip in her pocket, only to realize it was still in her room. With a second glance around the vacuous, empty menagerie, she walked to the console room to work, only to find that the network connection had been disabled.

She was just a girl, just an assistant, just another person traveling through space. Her skills wouldn't help her here.

She rested her head on her hands and waited.

Kat woke up sometime later. Her eyes cracked opened as a quiver ran down her body from the chill of the room. She lifted her head and winced, finding her neck tight and crooked, her arms red from leaning on them, and the groggy feeling of loss as sleep left her.

The light was dimmer than usual, lowered to accommodate that the day shift had ended. Bin-Three was a statue out of the corner of her eye. Kat stretched and stood up, turning to face her android guard.

She jerked and gasped as Dommik stepped out of the shadows instead, wearing nothing but a set of faded pants and his long, blue-black hair that fell over his chest. A stalker in the night. Her butt hit the table as he came upon her, his mouth hard and rough against her own. He caught her up against his chest as he set upon devouring her.

Kat was being eaten alive.

His heavy tongue thrust between her lips, demanding entrance. He licked her tongue, mimicking sex. Her body heated, readying for more, urged on by his thick bulge pressed into her stomach. Dommik jacked himself off with her entire frame.

The metal skeleton of his chest opened up, shifting and hot-as-hellfire to her skin, fraying her shirt off just as his second set of arms ripped it off her. Dommik leaned away to pull down her bra, thrusting her breasts up to his gaze, her nipples pert for his attention. Kat's eyes drifted down to his concave torso, no longer in its human shape.

She reached out to explore the metal inside him, the wires and the cords, where organs should have been but were not, having been replaced by parts.

He pulled the rest of her clothes off, shredding them until she stood there trembling in nothing but her bra. She reached forward to release his shaft.

"No." Dommik caught her hands and turned her around, he kicked her legs apart and bent her over the table. "What am I to do with my little fairy? She lost her wings along the way."

Kat shivered despite the heat of his body, her core already wet and ready enough to feel her essence drip down her thighs. One of his hands scraped down her back, two held her in place, gripping her hips.

Something warm touched her sex. "What're you doing!?"

It penetrated her, thin at first. *A finger?* Until it got thicker and wider. Curved and clawlike.

"Fairies don't get to speak," he snapped, clasping a hand over her mouth. "Goddamn, you're ready for me." He fucked his claw in and out of her, over and over, until it shifted inside of her, and left her at the mercy of two thick fingers pushing at her G-spot.

Kat arched her back and moaned into the hand clamped over her mouth, she stood on her tiptoes to relieve the pressure building inside. The hand on her back reached under to press into her pelvis, making her ready to explode. To squirm. To buckle.

185

"That's it," he said. She writhed under him, feeling him hook over her, his long hair tickling her back. "That's how a fairy gets her wings back." Her palms pressed into the table.

Kat screamed as she climaxed from his words.

Her body lit on fire as he forced his onslaught, pressing and pushing her, rounding her clit and pinching, milking every clench and moan from her soul.

And then his fingers were replaced by the sound of a rip and the hard rod of his dick. It conquered her. It destroyed her. It filled her to the brim and forced her submission.

The table shook beneath them as Dommik's thrusting lifted her butt up into the air, his body a shell hunkered over her, breaking her contact to everything but him. The console crushed under his hand and pushed to the side. Sparks flew with every forced fuck.

Kat rode the waves of her Cyborg.

She was vaguely aware after her second explosive orgasm, that her essence wasn't just her own anymore but a mixture of his seed and her priming. Her legs, the table, even the pads of her feet felt like they were slick with sex. Dommik kept cumming.

Kat moaned and let her control wilt to become his ragdoll. She pushed herself harder against him, taking her own pleasure.

She shrieked as another orgasmed was pulled from her just as she felt his body shift again. He changed while he fucked her. She braced as he pulled her to the floor and lifted her hips high up to display her core, her ass. Kat looked back to find a monster.

Dommik thrust back into her as her eyes roved over his outline. She saw four legs, four legs instead of two.

He took her again as his limbs pinned around her, trapping her in a pistoning cage. She closed her eyes and held onto a set of his wrists above her head. The prickle of sharp teeth raked across the back of her neck.

I'm-I'm being fucked by a monster. A spider...

She came again and collapsed into the embrace of eight limbs and the smell of sex, metal, and Dommik.

• • • •

HE NUZZLED HER NECK, her hair, her skin and lost himself into her erotic scent. He couldn't get enough of her. Dommik lifted her into his arms and pulled her close, relishing the feel of her soft body against his hard one. Kat looked up at him with hooded eyes, specks of green irises that could bring him to his knees, framed between long brown eyelashes.

She was everything he wanted, everything he had been searching for throughout the galaxies. His home, his world, his very life was held by her hands and by her words.

He had taken her like the beast he could be and saw the exact moment on her face when she realized the extent of the creature he was. And she had shattered from it.

Something roared in his head and drowned his heart. Katalina looked at him now with satiation and even a glint of mischief.

"I'm sorry," he groaned, pleased.

"I'm sorry too." She stared at him. "What're you hiding in the ship?"

Dommik laughed, "Myself." He shifted his second pair of legs back into him before she could get a real eyeful. The darkness could hide a lot, but it couldn't hide everything.

"I wish you would show me," she made a point of looking at his body. "I'm not easily scared away."

"Oh, I know, I'm not sure I could get rid of you even if I tried." He looked at her and stilled, knowing he had to tell her.

You're carrying my child. He couldn't bring himself to say it. *We can have children.* Dommik lifted her into his arms and walked them to the lavatory where he bathed them. *I bred you without you knowing...*

He watched his seed trickle over her thighs and go down the drain.

After they dried off, he took her to her quarters, where he uncharacteristically joined her in the small, single-sized bed. Their limbs twisted with a giggle and a grunt before they settled in. The bed held.

Kat poked and caressed his skin. "I can't find your seams. You're perfectly smooth. It's almost like you're an entirely different person...er...Cyborg when you change."

"I am. Were you scared?" he rubbed his chin over her wet curls.

"Startled, I don't know, shocked maybe? With everything that's happened, I'm pretty desensitized. I liked it. Seeing you like that. Have you shown yourself to others?"

"Yes, other Cyborgs, my doctors, men in the field. I usually worked alone, same with the others like me. We were designed as an afterthought," he spat the word out. "A theory and a test, a corruption of DNA, honing the right mind to control two forms."

"I don't see you as a corruption," she whispered into his neck.

"I'm a spider, Kat. You hate bugs."

"I don't hate you."

"If you cut me open, test my blood, check my scans, you'll find a myriad of spider genes attached to mine. I can even create my own poison." Dommik waited for her response, waited for her body to stiffen next to his, he waited for the horror that people who didn't *know* there were creations like him. The women soldiers on his ship tripping over themselves to run away from him, the men who felt like they had to target their commander with their guns, unsure for their lives. The first woman he took to bed, knowing what he was, cried to him afterward because she had lost a bet. "I make people sick by just the thought of me."

He felt her shrug and curl closer to him, Dommik couldn't get closer to her if he tried.

"You don't make me sick, you forced the sickness out of me, and demanded I move on. I'm trying." He felt her hand move down to grip something on her thigh, only to stop and relax. "I can't move on if I fear one bug for another. Will you show yourself to me someday? I'd like to see you. In the light, that is."

"Someday,"

"I'd like that. Mia is going to be so mad when we deliver her the flower and you haven't lost me."

"Maybe. Get some sleep. Tomorrow we'll reach out destination, but tonight I just want to hold you." He didn't want to hurt her, he wanted to keep her. His ears perked up at the soft sound of her breathing and his nostrils filled with their mutual scent. He felt perfection. Or the closest he had ever come to it in his long life.

Chapter Eighteen:

. . . .

Dommik left Kat at midnight Earthian time and went back to the bridge, keeping her door and the lavatory open for her use. He was covered in her scent and he relished it, knowing he took a little piece of her with him when he left.

Bin-One, his constant companion, was waiting for him when he arrived.

"Report."

"The Trentian aircraft is still tailing us, Master. They have informed nearby ships not to interfere with your passage," it responded.

"What about our destination?" Dommik sat at the helm, pulling up the coordinates.

"We will be within Xan'Mara's atmosphere in the next hour. Shall I find us a port to land, Master?"

He looked out over the dark room, eyeing the ropes he had hanging throughout his makeshift web in every corner. It was varying, thick in some places while others were just knotted heaps and bundles. Matted hair with wet and dripping fibers that almost touched the ground. He found a length and tugged it into his hands, enjoying the burn as it chafed across his skin.

"No, I'll find us a place. Thank you, Bin-One, you can go below." It left without a farewell.

Dommik checked his transmissions, finding only several from Mia and the EPED hailing him for his status, and one from Gunner.

'Arrived at Xan'Mara, day 22th of May, with an escort from Space Lord Markoss to retrieve one O'lia flower.'

It wouldn't arrive before he was done with this mission. Messages were slow this far out in space. He expected they would be on their way home by the end of the day. He opened the security feed to see that Kat hadn't moved from her quarters.

He opened Gunner's message.

'Stryker's a real dumbass who's going to get himself fried. I need you to take my deliveries in. I'll meet you at the spot.'

Dommik chose not to respond. He didn't want Gunner to know his current coordinates. If Gunner entered Trentian airspace, the aliens had an allowance to take him in and take him out without a reason. He wasn't about to get mixed up with political warfare. It was his least favorite kind.

The moon came into view and he scanned the surface for the pilgrims, finding several settlements throughout the muddy-grey landscape. The surface reminded him of stagnant puddles of water left behind by the sun's rays to birth new bugs.

The flower, a native to the moon, was harvested and sold by the pilgrims as their main source of income. It was often used for medicinal purposes for the aliens, as well as having a vitality boost upon intake, a natural steroid that could increase energy and endurance. It was a symbol in bonding pairs to be taken before mating to prolong the act and guarantee that insemination had occurred.

It was an outdated ritual that had come back in recent years. A small hope to replenish the Trentian species after the war and the breeders disease.

Earth wanted it.

One flower. One is all you get.

Dommik was sure the Space Lord believed he couldn't keep the flower alive to bring one back. But he was going to damned well try just to spite the bastard. Even so, it was hard to care about anything anymore, his mind lost since Argo and now his heart was bleeding out of him every time he thought about Kat.

And the child he put in her womb. His nanocells reconfiguring and bonding to her egg to create a human baby. Cyborgs can't be born, but the child he gave her would be superior to any human alive.

Except for the monstrous qualities his father had...the blood of bugs.

He only hoped that Kat would see it as she saw him. And someday forgive him.

Dommik looked down at his hands to find the rope tied tight into a ball. He threw it to his web, where it got caught in the strands. The ship screened the atmosphere and alerted him for landing. A flat plateau of land within a wild field of plants. He felt his ship adjust as he left the bridge.

He buckled up in light armor that was camouflaged and strengthened with his specific bio-suits nanoparticles. The knives he kept and his specialized darts were tucked into the bands of his suit, with one pistol for good measure.

193

Who knows what that flower could do. He found himself snickering as he entered the elevator, checking the metal parts of his body to ensure safe shifting. Nothing stuck.

He was good to go.

Dommik ran into Kat as the elevator opened. She softened under his gaze, greeting him with a yawn and stretch. Her tits perked as they pressed into the soft cloth of her shirt.

She eyed him back. "Time to pluck the flower?"

Dommik wanted to shift back into his beast and fuck her all over again. "I've already plucked it," he growled, pulling her against him. "You should be holding onto something during landing." The ship shuddered as he said it.

"Good thing I have you to keep me in line." She leaned up and kissed the underside of his jaw.

More blood dripped from his heart.

"They know we're here. Let's get this over with."

• • • •

KAT LEANED UP ON HER toes and placed a kiss on Dommik's cheek. They were on Xan'Mara and had passed the first test brought on by the Trentians. One flower, only one flower could be extracted because of her. Kat should have stayed at Ghost. She didn't know how they were going to get the plant back to Earth, alive. All she could think of to do was kiss him and continue kissing him. Hoping each kiss would make him forgive her faster, love her faster. She flinched.

"Be safe."

"It's a damned flower."

194

"And it changed our lives." He turned to face her, his eyes hard. "This isn't Argo," she whispered.

"You don't even know. You should have stayed on Ghost."

Kat sighed, exasperated. "I know. And if the flower dies, I'll lose my job anyway, right?"

Dommik looked at her like he knew something. Something she didn't. "You don't even know." He dropped down on his knees and lifted her shirt, his lips kissing her right below her belly button. She grabbed his hair for balance as his breath tickled her into a shuddering frenzy. He stood up with a twisted smile that she couldn't help smile back at. "I'll be back soon. It's a failed mission if it dies. We only get one."

He stepped away from her and entered the hull, but she followed as he checked the edge of one of his knives. One gun strapped to his hip. Kat looked at the weapons at length and the weapon he *was*. She knew on some level that he would never hurt her, that in a way she may have been the only person he would never hurt. That's if she could believe the whispers he flooded into her ear the night before.

Kat shook herself, "Then steal some seeds. Did he say anything about the seeds?"

His steps echoed in her ears and she knew he was withdrawing into his metal shell. The hard exterior of his body solidified and his eyes darkened into the shadows they were. Dommik unraveled his humanity, leaving nothing but the Monster Hunter he was behind.

The hatch opened up, letting a waft of earthy soil into the ship, pervading the once sanitized space. She gulped it down as if Heaven itself was just through that door.

The Trentian ship landed with a plume just outside, killing the fresh smell with exhaust and fire. Kat tried to peer around Dommik, but he shielded her sight. "If I'm not back in twenty-four hours, alert Mia and the EPED. Don't open the hatch for anyone." He stared at the other ship, his voice no longer human.

"I won't." *Can I even open the hatch?*

The door shut with him on the other side. And silence met her every breath. She looked up at the vents that groaned on above. The smell of everything outside her cage disappeared into the ceiling as if it had never been there to begin with.

One of the Bins approached her. "He left this for you, Katalina Jones." The android handed her a wristlet.

"Thank you," she said, putting it on. It didn't help the feeling of suffocation.

Kat walked back to the elevator to see if it would open but to her annoyance, it did not. Checking the console room only made her heart race; the computer was gone, smashed and cleaned up by the androids. Before long she found herself pacing back and forth across the menagerie, counting every step and every second that passed.

The door to the roach room loomed in her periphery and every time she came close to it, her steps quickened. Every time she noticed it, fear clouded her mind. It was as if the room was alive and waiting for her and it watched her with hunger.

Kat could *feel* it watch her. She could also feel her promise cracking under the pressure of its gaze, reminding her of the sickness that killed her parents and the delusions she fed from it.

Until her feet faltered and she stood in front of it. The door peeled open, allowing her entry. *What were the odds that the very thing I feared most was with me this whole time...*

Kat stepped through the innocuous rectangular entryway and into the light where she was going to face her fears. Not for Dommik, but for herself.

Chapter Nineteen:

• • • •

Dommik ignored the Piercer and crept to the high stalks that ran flush and far over the endless fields on either side of him. They were stiff and stubborn, the type of plant that made great padding for dens, burrows, and nests for birds, but he didn't see any immediate wildlife about him. He never did when he first landed on a planet. His ship would scare everything away.

The shadow of his spacecraft towered over him, blocking out the twin suns on the horizon. The colors of the day were moving fast, and the moon was small, meaning he would encounter the night soon. Dommik walked over the plants, pummeling them down under his boots only to have them spring back up behind him as if he had never passed through. He checked his wrist-con and followed its compass to the nearest settlement, a half-league away.

He hoped, which was something Cyborgs Did Not Do, that he could buy a flower straight from the source, alive, dug up with roots and all.

He didn't have alien currency on hand, coins forged deep within the tunnels on Xanteaus Trent, but he did have things to barter. That hope was only brought on by a bone-deep urge to get this job done and get Kat someplace safe.

Someplace they could both heal together.

Dommik looked back at the two ships in the distance, checking the landscape and listening to the breeze. No one was following him, which was just as well. If Markoss sent a scout after him, he would have to keep that peon alive.

He reached down and untied his boots, setting them aside in the rushes before he shifted his lower body. He counted to ten, his bio-suit reformed, down to five, tied back his hair and ended at one.

Dommik sprinted, low to the ground and out of sight toward his destination.

There was no sound but the rush of wind over his face and no one to see him but the suns in the sky, damning him and judging his form. Time slipped by as he closed in on his destination, minutes only, while his body ran with four legs, skittering with metal close to the ground.

He stopped short when his destination appeared. His extra limbs twisted back into hiding while he took cover at the edge of the stalks. He peeked through the gaps.

Pillars and a hole. Nothing more although he knew there were others. He checked his surroundings, finding it clear, and stepped out into the light.

The hole slipped into the darkness at an angle and, as he got closer, he saw that there was a staircase made out of stone that led deep within. Small white globes sat on the sides. They illuminated every step.

Dommik stared up at the sky. *Always underground. Always fucking underground.* He wasn't the type of spider that thrived in the dirt, especially after his past experiences.

He should've known the settlements would be away from the sun and the heat of the day. The aliens couldn't tolerate heat; they thrived in the cold. Their blood would slowly boil until they cooked and collapsed. Xanteaus Trent, their homeworld, was farther away from their sun and they adapted to accommodate it, just like humans had for their relatively temperate environment.

Dommik stepped down into the hole until he was swallowed up by the terra. His fingers flexed over his knife. By the time it leveled out he had an audience of a hundred staring at him.

"I come in peace," He shouted, feeling like a space-age idiot. Two men draped in green pants, woven by the stalks above approached him, their chests bare except for designs knifed into their skin brought out by scars. He didn't need to look around to know there were no women present.

If they had women, it wouldn't be here. The wood smelled of mold, the rocks uncarved, and the cavern in its entirety reeked of sweat and rot.

"Yhal en Erarth. Pucha ere?" one of the two said in Trentian. Dommik closed his eyes and subsumed his inclination to kill the aliens back deep within himself and switched to Trentian. *You're from Earth. Why are you here?*

"I'm here to buy a flower."

The same one spoke and his head rolled as he considered him. "We don't sell to humans. We don't negotiate with filth."

"The Space Lord I came here with said you would." Dommik didn't mind name-dropping if it got him out of there faster. He placed his hand on his knife's handle.

"We don't follow the sect that lost this war and tainted our blood," the alien bared his teeth, followed by the hundred still staring at them baring their teeth. "They have no jurisdiction amongst the pure."

"Unfortunately for you, your moon lies within that *sect's* jurisdiction."

Dommik felt the change before it started, the rustle of beings all focused on their weapons, the one that was easily within reach. A target for one's mind and the stiffening of muscles a moment before. He kept his eyes on the man before him.

"Xanteaus has forsaken them, his voice no longer fills their heads. We are here to rise up and take the impure down and restore the god's star in pure soil. You taint holy ground, outsider."

Dommik looked out calmly over the aliens, their bared bodies strained, their hands cupped and unclothed. Each an unlit wick waiting for the fire. Unconcerned hatred marred their faces.

"Markoss didn't tell you I was coming, did he?"

Several of the aliens closest to him stopped.

A trap?

He continued, "You don't have to die. I'll walk out of here and you'll never see me again. One flower, with the roots still intact, is all I ask for." The snake hiss of daggers being unsheathed filled his ears. "I'm not interested in war." The aliens started to slink around him.

The sweat of impending battle stunk up the globe-glowed cavern.

"We will sacrifice you to Xanteaus, the god of gods and the star within the first world. There will be no accursed here!"

He let his Trentian kill-code arise and allowed the poison to build up in his system.

The alien savages expected a slaughter, and it looked like they were going to get one. Not the one they wanted, though. He turned into the metal monster that he was and let the venom that bubbled up from his body secrete from his elongated teeth and from his fingertips.

He slashed and cut, dripping with rancor and vitriol, and soon the slop of alien blood as the first wave came at him. His legs came apart and then the real slaughter began.

It wasn't until he climbed the cavern walls and sprayed down his poison that the screams took on a whole new pitch.

He left bodies in his wake, some dead, most nearly dead as they succumbed to the acid in their veins and the paralysis. The aliens on the outskirts, untouched, began to back away while the brave began to shoot him down with bullets that ricocheted off his exoskeleton.

For every alien that dropped, two more took its place, and he had yet to enjoy the carnage. His joints popped and his mouth pulled out until it broke away from his face while the bones of his canines shifted underneath, soaking up the poison that was left over, and replaced with razor sharp steel.

Dommik let his control vanish in the battle cries and the spears that poked at his Cyborg body and dropped down on a horde of aliens, crushing their bodies under his heavy frame.

"Drop the dirt!"

"For the god of gods!"

He tore at their throats and roared with a mouth full of blood until the Trentians backed away. A rumble shook the ground followed by the stone floor cracking open. The dead and dying began to tremble and slip away as the wails of the aliens turned to cheers.

His limbs shook as the jagged crevasse came for him. He jumped back but stumbled over the pliant bodies littering his escape. The small ray of sun from the entrance began to disappear. A gate closing in from the sides.

Dommik speared his lower half into the wall when the entire floor opened up into a black hole. The Trentians around the edges continued to berate him with bullets and throwing spears, and he even felt the sting of rocks.

Fucking hell. His spider legs slipped down the stone and with the rumble of the floor closing up, he fell into the pit.

Chapter Twenty:

• • • •

If there was one thing Dommik knew, it was that he didn't have a perfect record; as a Cyborg, he was perfectly imperfect.

He cursed the EPED when he landed on two of his legs, crushing them beneath his heavy frame. He then cursed Stryker for *having* a perfect record; that bastard always took the cushy jobs.

If he deployed a distress call, how many would ignore it before it was too late?

His body sparked as he assessed the damage, finding the two limbs next to useless. They pulled at his body, keeping him off balance and frustrated.

Dommik slipped his fingers across the crushed appendage, bending it toward him until it was close enough for coverage all while fighting off the pain. Because he did feel pain. Even with his nanocells programmed to heal him at a rapid rate and his natural tolerance toward it, he felt pain. It caught him up like quicksand, from the torn apart tendons to the bullet-ridden flesh, slowly sinking him into its pit.

He lay back amongst the corpses, listening to the last dying hushes of those he doomed around him, and waited until the final death breath whispered into his ear.

I have to get back to Kat.

The sparks died out, sputtering into the dirt and the blood. He lifted his arm and turned on his wrist-con and looked around. The light didn't go far, but he could tell he was in a cavern larger than the last, colder than the last, and there was life skittering around him. He waited for his eyes to adjust into night vision.

There were plants and small rodent-like creatures, blinded, and bugs–always bugs–coming to feast on the dead.

He sat up and looked closer, holding his arm out before his face. The body next to him twitched.

And then he felt it...something under him poking up from the ground like needles. His neighbor's torso sucked inward as if something was slurping it from the inside-out, and it sounded as such.

Fuck. Dommik lifted himself to his feet and moved away. He wasn't going to stay and watch when he could be its next meal. His circuits fired with each footstep, sending tiny jolts to his limbs. It was several yards of dragging before he stepped off the dead and onto the ground, the light of his tech leading the way.

His foot sank into the wet soil; the ground sucked at his every step.

Dommik gritted his teeth and looked down.

He saw the flowers.

Drifting toward the pile of gore with needle-like vines, sucking out the blood.

He stopped and watched, dazed as he began to actually sink. And as the wafts of putrid waste that had marinated for an eternity wrecked his senses, the flowers dined. The sound of a hundred footfalls echoed above him where the floor had opened up.

So this is their secret. Carnivorous flowers. There had been no mention about the flower itself in the missive, only the ritual and perceived properties taken from the Trentians and the half-breeds that bought them. The real bloom wasn't even supposed to exist.

He stepped farther away from the pile and located several flowers amongst the outskirts, unhindered by blood or crushed by bodies and metal, and appropriated one from the muck. It fought him with barbs and twisted like a snake in his hand. Carefully, he pulled it away from the floor, mindful of the gooping roots as he opened up a container under his arm.

A roach-like creature scuttled between the petals.

Dommik marveled at it for a moment before sticking both creatures away.

Time to go home.

If the flowers are down there, it meant there had to be a way out. An entrance and exit for the harvest. He waved his wrist-con above him and looked at the closest wall. He followed it with each lumbering step. The flowers and bugs paid him no mind, their focus on the easy meal of corpses in the center.

When he found a carved out ladder, gouged into the wall with intermittent hand-supports, he climbed it to the top, hauling the incredible weight of his broken legs behind him. His fingers dug into the stone as another jolt went through his systems, causing him to jerk and nearly fall. Something was sizzling inside him.

His tech could get wet, it was built to withstand the elements, but his tech couldn't get crushed *and* wet. He was on the edge of short-circuiting, and was going to fry.

Dommik gritted his teeth and kept going. He reached a shallow landing several meters up that led to a closed stone door. He lay on his back and took a long, frustrated breath, before he broke the ground with his hands and gripped the bottom of the slat. He put his muscle into it and heaved the door up until he had enough room to crawl beneath it, pivoting and ducking his useless limbs through first.

He found himself in a dark tunnel that curved out of sight.

On either side sat half-empty crates and strung up animal carcasses being drained of blood. He tried not to smell; he tried instead to imagine fresh air and Kat's erotic scent, but the rot was pervasive and forced its way inside. It left him feeling hungry for blood of his own.

His broken legs ground out the path behind him as he crept along, and they screeched and thundered, creating their own echoes off of the walls. He didn't try to be quiet. It would've been too much effort.

Before long the Trentians joined him in the shadows and fed his bloodlust. Each death brought him closer to turning off his humanity.

Each kill made him crazed. Crazed for violence and sex. Blood and rope, and his fairy waiting for him to take her.

A lever filled his vision. It stuck out of the stone wall at an angle. His eyes twitched and flashed as he ran for it.

An alarm rang as he re-entered the cavern, and released the floor. It was too late for the savages caught in their own trap.

The rest he killed with his claws.

• • • •

KAT HEARD THE ANDROIDS first. Then she heard the hatch.

Her first instinct was to stay calm and peek around the corner, in case someone besides her Cyborg overrode the ship's systems.

"Master Dommik."

Her second instinct was running to him and flying into his arms, taking the flower from his hands and potting it in the botany enclosures, all while kissing and preparing for take-off. That was playing through her head as she hurried after the androids.

Kat stopped short as the door opened to a gore-covered broken pile of man and metal. Not the man she had pictured. She recoiled as familiar black eyes peered up at her under a face covered in foul smelling grime.

It's wrong. Kat gagged. *No...*

He fell forward, scraping limbs against the silver floor. She jumped back and flinched away from the screeches, from the monster dragging forward.

"Kat," he groaned.

No. No, please no. She barely stopped herself from retching.

The androids surrounded it and tried to lift the broken machine into the ship.

"Dommik?" she asked, afraid of the spindly robot in front of her. His head fell forward under the weight of his hair, dripping brown sludge. "Dommik," she

208

cried and gripped his face, finding his eyes again amongst the odd metal extruding from his jaw, the metallic teeth pointing up. "Oh my God, what happened to you?"

He twitched and jerked and she felt the shock in her hands. He didn't answer. His entire body seized and crackled.

"Okay. Okay," she breathed. "You're safe now. I'm going to make you better." Kat put herself under one of his arms and helped the Bins drag him into the ship. They made it half a foot before he collapsed, bringing them with him.

"Dommik! Wake up, WAKE UP!" She contorted her body and cupped his face. "You have to help us get you to medical. Dommik!" Screaming at him when he didn't move. "Please wake up."

Kat joined the androids again in pulling him forward. "Come on, come on. Come-fucking-on!" She unhooked herself and gripped his arm, trying to pull now with the Bins. "You're," she hissed, "So," she leaned back, "Fucking," Kat fell on her ass, "*Heavy*."

Her hands came away covered in only-gods-know-what something that smelled of sour sulfur.

She got back up and tried again, screaming expletives the whole time. Kat begged him to wake up, changing tactics and finding water to pour on his face, but he didn't.

The Bins on either side of her continued at it with a calm assurance that she wished she had.

Sparks flew off several of his lower limbs and as she moved to get a closer look at the damage, a roar filled her ears.

Not a roar. Kat stiffened, terrified, and looked out the hatch. "That's not wind," she whispered, her eyes noticing the other damage her Cyborg had endured. Slashed skin and burned holes.

Kat struggled to her feet and grabbed the pistol that was still attached to Dommik's unmoving side and ducked out into the open landscape and ran toward the alien's ship.

"Open up!" she threw herself at the side, tears trickling down her face. "Help me! Markoss. Help me, please!"

Kat pounded at the side of the large spacecraft, knocking the gun against the unmovable wall, spurred on by adrenaline. She didn't leave a dent nor a mark, and her screams and psychotic worry went unheard between the ships.

"Goddamnit." Her body fell into the alien ship and slid down its side. The sound of encroaching battle grew closer.

She wiped at her face and fumbled with the gun, unsure on how to use it, but finding the safety nevertheless and turned it off. With her body trembling from exertion and her palms damp with sweat, she held the heavy firearm out before her and watched as the field of stalks began to sway and shake; waiting for whatever, whoever would break through the plant wall.

Kat ducked behind a sharp cone of metal and screamed, "If you don't fucking help me, Markoss, I will destroy you. If Dommik dies..." she hesitated, waiting, and whispered to herself, "If he dies, I'll kill you all." She felt the rage in her words. She believed in it although she knew she wasn't going to make it out of this alive.

The first men ran through the edge and stopped, taking in the giant metal ships they came to attack. Kat lifted her gun and aimed.

The recoil jerked her hand. She missed and aimed again. Her muscles tensed and she shot off several rounds. One target went down wailing.

They saw her location and started running for her, their bodies becoming a swarm as they appeared from the field. Another went down. She shot at them until her gun clicked empty. *Fuck, fuck, fuck.*

Kat ducked behind the metal wall and took a deep breath. Her heart wanted her to run, to hide, but her mind and body were ready to fight. She crept back toward the edge, bracing to pounce, her eyes wandering back at the open hatch where her Cyborg lay unmoving and the androids who continued to try to get him inside.

The first Trentian rushed by. She leapt onto him, tearing at his skin and bringing him to the ground. She struggled to get the dagger he wielded.

But then he slumped on top of her, dead.

Kat's eyes filled with rainbows as the body was lifted away. She caught a hold of Markoss just before he unsheathed his diamond scythe and she went blind. He gripped her shirt and half threw her back behind the metal cone, berating her, "A pregnant woman should be nowhere near a battlefield, Katalina."

When her sight came back, it came with the spray of blood, and a dozen aliens dead beside her.

Dazed, she barely comprehended the alien's words. They were crazy. Dommik must have lied to the Trentian so they wouldn't abduct her. She didn't look back at the Space Lord, still blinking out the blind spots she incurred. Her hands found the dagger and ran back to Dommik. She covered him until the battle cries vanished and a chant she couldn't understand replaced it.

"It's going to be okay now," she said, protecting his shell. Markoss and a band of aliens appeared, the crystal scythe once again put away. Kat held up her dagger. "If you want him, you have to go through me first."

The Trentians stared at her.

"You have beautiful green eyes."

Chapter Twenty-One:

• • • •

Markoss and several of his guards carried Dommik into the ship. Kat led them up to the medbay, using his metal frame to open the previously locked doors.

She didn't trust the aliens and watched them warily. They set Dommik on the medical slab, where the Bins began to work on his broken metal, repairing him piece by small piece.

A compartment opened up at the back of the room for the Bins, housing everything a Cyborg could need for emergency assistance, down to low-grade replacement limbs and circuit boards.

Kat got to work cleaning his wounds, stripping him of his dirty suit, and sewing up the deeper gashes. She ran a cleaning cloth over every inch of him, every piece and part of his eight limbs, all while Markoss sat and watched her from the corner. Silent and eerie.

It was hard for her to breathe with him drilling his eyes into her soul.

This is not what I imagined.

One of the androids opened up a box, spilling forth a writhing flower and a bug that skittered across the floor. Kat jumped back as the flower crawled to her.

"What the...?"

Markoss picked it up and examined it. "An O'lia flower, a real one. How intriguing."

Kat looked at the bloody thing in his hand. "What do you mean a real one?"

"We harvested them to extinction centuries ago, Katalina."

"I don't understand?"

Markoss found a container and placed the flower within, slicing his hand to drip blood over its roots. Intrigued, Kat watched as the thing drank it and bulged up. Markoss placed a top on it.

"Katalina, Lina, the real O'lia were thought to be extinct. The stuff on the market now is a cheap imitation to satisfy the ritual. But this one is real, Katalina, very interesting."

"You knew and you didn't tell us?"

"Why would I?"

Yeah, why would he? Kat counted to five. Then counted to five again.

She followed the roach with a sigh and trapped it within her hands, placing it within the container that jailed the vampiric flower. She watched as it settled on the stem before wiping her hands clean. Her attention returned back to Markoss, the alien, where he hovered at her side, towering like Dommik.

"I don't know if I should thank you or kill you," she said.

"Neither. I deserve neither." He bowed his head and went back to his spot in the corner.

Kat moved to sit at her Cyborg's side and settled in to watch his body heal and the androids work their magic. When there was nothing left to do but wait, she found sleep with her head resting on one his arms.

When her eyes fluttered open sometime later, feeling movement under her cheek, she lifted up to a body crooked and aching with pain and a stomach full of cramps. The first thing she noticed was Dommik's limbs shifting. The second thing was that Markoss was gone.

Only one android remained and she knew it was Bin-Three. The metal spider turned back into a man with a ticking and a creak. Gone was the fluid silence of his movement. His eyes didn't open.

"Is he going to be okay?" she asked the bot.

"Master Dommik is restarting. He is okay."

"How long?"

"Twenty-four minutes and three seconds until completion."

"Thank you." She massaged the back of her neck. A sheet was placed over Dommik's nudity when his extra limbs fully vanished inside his shell.

"Here is your dinner." Bin-Three handed her a nutrition bar. Kat took it with a smile. *Routine feels good.* She placed it on the table next to her knocking her knuckles into a reader.

Her reader.

The one that had beeped.

Kat grabbed it and turned it on. She closed her eyes to find her buried courage, fear strangled her heart and closed up her throat. *I'm fine. I don't have the parasite. I can't have it. I'm vaccinated. I don't have it.* Her body broke out into a cold sweat.

"Katalina, dear, nothing in life comes easy. You'll find that your demons come back over and over. What you do about those visits is entirely up to you. Exorcising a demon is as hard as forgetting a memory."

She opened her eyes and read her results.

● ● ● ●

DOMMIK WOKE UP ALONE. Not alone. His eyes landed on the Trentian standing at the foot of his bed. His skin was cold, but his metal interior burned him up from the inside. He flexed his muscles, registering his extra limbs locked within.

The next instant he had his metal claw around the alien's throat, drawing blood. "What happened?" he growled.

The Space Lord remained still. "You came back broken. Katalina, Talina, and your robots repaired you, Dommik."

"Did you touch her?" Venom rose up into his mouth.

"I did not."

"Where is she? If she has come to any harm, I'll kill you slowly, painfully, and your entire crew. And gift your corpses to the flowers."

"Dommik, she is fine, shaken up, but here. Katalina took your prize and is housing it in an enclosure as we speak."

Dommik threaded through his androids and saw her through their eyes down below. He stole their recordings of the last day away and uploaded them into his drives. It took him all of several seconds to review the material.

Her screams, her cries as she tried to get him inside. Taking his weapon and calling for help, shooting at the remaining pilgrims, and of Markoss and his men slaughtering them. He saw Kat crouch over him with a knife, preparing to fight to the death. For him.

216

The surgery, the cleanup, her conversation with the Space Lord, the flower, and he saw her find the reader.

Dommik kept his hold around Markoss's neck and checked the stitches on his arms and chest, already fading away. His eyes landed on the reader across the room.

He let the Trentian go. "Get off my ship."

Markoss canted his head, twisting his lips. "She loves you."

Dommik pulled out clothes from the cybernetics cabinet and dressed. "Get. Off. My. Ship. I don't like liars, Markoss." Throwing his words back at him.

The creeping chill of the Space Lord's laugh could have given lesser men night terrors. It wheezed low and heavy until it filled his ears, the breeze before the storm.

All he cared about was getting to Kat, talking to her, forcing her to accept him, and kissing her into compliance before he yelled at her for putting herself into harm's way.

"Before I go, I want to thank you, Dommik. Dommik, thank you for killing the heretics. Xanteaus would not allow me to kill them until they drew first blood." He ended on a patronizing final "Dommik," before he vanished outside the door.

Dommik followed after him, only to find the passageway empty. He continued down through each door wedged open and kicked them closed behind him. Kat and his androids were down below, placing the O'lia flower away with the roach still alive and well on it.

He stormed past them and went to the still-opened hatch, closing it to a scene of countless Trentians readying to reap Xan'Mara with its own inquisition. Heralded by a thousand splintering rainbows.

"Bin-One, ready us for take-off," he called out. "We're headed for Earth."

He felt the chinks and gaps in his frame as he approached Kat, who looked at everything and nothing except him.

"You're covered in filth."

"Thank you for your observation. I know that already." She turned to walk away.

"We need to talk," he followed her.

"Not right now." She stopped at the door to her quarters. It didn't open.

"Yes, right now. You're upset and you could be hurt. You need to go to medical."

Kat turned to him, launching into a spit-fire rage as she started to hit him, pummel him, claw at him in any and every way that she could, screaming all the while. He let her use him, let her cry and hit him until the furor simmered to anger. Until her body shook with exhaustion.

She leaned her forehead on his chest and he reached up to pet her hair, "You knew. You knew and didn't tell me. Why?" she asked, her voice hoarse.

"I didn't want you to hate me," Dommik sighed.

"When? How did it happen?" She trembled against him. "How did it happen? I haven't slept with anyone but you. Wh–who raped me?" Her words broke into pieces.

My heart bleeds.

He cupped her face and forced her to look up at him. "No one raped you, Kat." And caught her tears with his fingers. "It's mine. Ours." His hold on her tightened. "I would never let anyone harm you. Never. You're mine, forever, whether you accept it or not. You chose me and I took you. I would–will destroy any man who touches you."

Dommik willed her to look at him, willed her back to him, willed whatever they had between them to survive. He needed her to see the emotion in his emotionless eyes. *Maybe I ask too much.*

"I chose the job over Ghost, not you and not this baby. You've taken all my choices away," she hissed, pulling herself out of his arms. "I hate you!" Kat moved away from him and stood next to her door, waiting to be let into her room. "Please, please just let me go. I can't think. I can't feel, I can't feel anything. I'm numb! You made me numb!" Her hands closed into fists at her side with the gleam to strike him again. He was ready to take whatever she gave him.

"Kat..." *I don't know what to say.*

"You don't get to call me that, not anymore!" Instead, she hit the door and screamed. "I hate you. I hate you. I hate you! You are a monster!" Each word accompanied with the loud thunk of vibrating aluminum.

Dommik's eyes narrowed as she retreated from him physically, mentally, the wild look of her gone and the green dimmed to dust in her irises. Her clothes soiled and torn, dirt and dried blood on her skin, and the copper curls now straight and plastered to her face. "No," he reached for her and pushed her against the wall where he devoured her unresponsive mouth until she devoured him back. "No."

They fed off the chaos. He fed on his desperation. She bit his lip and took his violence. Dommik gave her everything with rage, his metal body, and his soul.

He pinned her, pressing hard, needing to feel every curve and contour of her body against his and felt her hands reach between them and tug at his pants. He peeled hers off as she worked his down. Her hands found his tightening cock and gripped it.

"No," he growled and ground himself into her. Kat tugged at his hair sending prickles through him. Dommik smelled her arousal as his fingers dipped between her legs to find her clit.

"I need," she threw her head back. "I need..."

"What do you need?" He rubbed her in sure, slow strokes, finding his own pleasure as she buckled.

"To come, please," she panted. "I thought you were dead. I hate you."

Dommik lifted her and hooked her legs around him, while she held on as he returned to her pussy, her pussy that clenched around his fingers as he penetrated it, rubbing her G-spot and scissoring to stretch her tight walls to take him. He was desperate to get inside of her, to fill her up, to fuck her wet slit into oblivion.

To be the only insect within her, to be the only parasite she had to endure. He was it, he was hers.

"I hate you," she said again as he replaced his hand with the thick head of his cock.

"I know." He sank into her slowly, coveting every inch she gave him and he took. It was too much. To explosive. And too close to the brink of pain for

220

either of them. She embraced him and held on as he filled her with every single inch. When they reached the apex, all sense left them, and a frenzy took its place.

He bottomed out inside of her.

Dommik ravaged her against the wall, bumping and jerking, as she screamed into his mouth and he swallowed them up. Sliding her wet sheath over him with each thrust all while he repeated, *No no no.*

They came together as he picked her up and held her in his arms, watching her lose herself riding his bulge with no leverage but his body. He watched as his fairy rode out her climax in mid-air. Each used the other for their own gratification.

It was over before it had begun and the high of uncontrollable desire dissipated, leaving them quiet and cold in each other's arms. In a pact, silent, and brooding while they both tried to hold onto the fantasy for a minute longer. A second. Their bodies flushed and overheated.

Kat's legs unhooked. She slipped from his arms and tucked her hair behind her ears, "I hate you," she repeated again softly. "I want to hate you. I need to hate you." She kicked her pants and hugged herself. "So, please, just let me hate you."

Dommik watched as she drifted away from him, leaving a thousand words unspoken. He reached past her and opened her quarters. Her eyes became hooded as she stepped inside.

"Kat," he took a step after her and laid his heart on his sleeve. "I'm sorry."

"I know." And the door shut.

Chapter Twenty-Two:

• • • •

T hey left Xan'Mara that day. They left it to its
bloodbath, battles, and civil war, knowing who the
victor was before it even began. The screams of battle
cries in the gust of their wake and the explosion of
rainbows in their memory.

Dommik took a long drag from one of his stashed
cigars and savored the earthy flavor, releasing the
puff into the air where it vanished within the
ventilation. After he left Kat, he had Bin-Three
deliver her a new wristlet, one that had access to the
entirety of the ship.

He waited for her to find him, letting her make the
choice to remain or go, forcing himself to give up
some of his control. He didn't know what to do,
because all of it was unfamiliar territory.

They left Trentian airspace less than a week later,
passing through the invisible walls of one sector to
another, drifting through the grey in-between until
reentering home territory. The Earthian zone of
control was a general third of the galaxy and was only
distinguished by who ruled what port, planet, and
colony on the outskirts. Disregarding those few places
where the two species ruled in equal measure.

A week.

Every minute that went by drove him a little
crazier. He waited for her to wander, to test out where
the wristlet worked, to regain a modicum of curiosity

back, but she didn't. She kept to her regimen and far away from him. Dommik wanted her to see the engraved, *forever yours*, on the inside.

A week left him burning through cigars, and repairing the parts of him that stuck. He opened his tech and tweaked his circuits, cleaned up his wires, and reforged the metal pieces that didn't match up. He worked tirelessly when she was off-shift, taking care of the creatures on board, cutting off the requests the EPED made and answering them himself during the break.

He fed the flower blood each night.

And put his new roach in its own enclosure.

When he found himself storming to confront her, lurking in the corners out of her line of sight, feeding his want by eating her up with his eyes, he would tear into his man-made webbing and rip it to shreds. He would then pick up the pieces and retie them back together.

Dommik had never felt more imprisoned. Not even when he was buried underground on a dead world.

He watched her from the shadows. He watched her eyes regain some of their gleam, the soft blush of her flesh find its color again, her copper curls growing out to drift over her shoulders. He watched and yearned as she tried to converse with his androids, he watched her observing the creatures thriving in their habitats, he watched as she worked. Every sigh she released was his, every stretch, every time her fingers brushed through her hair. He watched.

Until his *need* grew into something animalistic, something possessive bordering a dark path he did not want to go down, but it called to him anyway, every day.

A week became two and each day lasted an eternity, each second a crazed agony. They were due to arrive at Earth within the next fortnight, pending any last minute missions.

He extinguished his cigar and tried to contact Stryker, again, only to receive no answer, and finding no answer nor call back from Gunner, he became worried.

The EPED had notified him both agents had gone silent within the last several weeks. They hadn't given Dommik a search and rescue mission as of yet, but it had come to the point that he was going after them after the drop-off.

They hadn't died, which he knew because he was still able to locate their IP addresses when seeding through the network. They were just *not answering.* He didn't like being out of the loop if something major was going down.

At least it would get my mind off of her. Dommik scowled. *Off of everything.*

Patience had never been a virtue with which he struggled. That was the spider in him; however, it was getting harder and harder to deal with her absence. He turned back to his ropes and wove a new web across the bridge.

He was stiff, on edge, and at the pinnacle of his own destruction when the security feed flashed. Her presence moved toward the elevator. He let go of the frayed rope and watched.

Finally.

• • • •

KAT FELT COLD AS SHE twisted her new wristlet around, keeping her hand busy while she surfed the network and passed her time. She would've continued to drum her fingers except that they felt bruised and tender from so much typing.

She read up on anything and everything that presented itself. There was always some "new" breakthrough, a new planet that was habitable, a new cure, new technology, and sometimes there was a tragic death of someone important, murders, a smuggling ring brought down.

Nothing kept her attention anymore.

What she didn't find was any news about the aliens, what they were doing, what was happening on the other side of the galaxy. Sure, there were the broad strokes, dignitaries shaking hands, and reform for the half-breeds, but she found next to nothing about the Space Lords, and nothing about rebel sects and internal fighting.

Kat tensed. Her back stiffened and she knew she was being watched. She tried not to look around and find him, because she didn't want to see him.

I don't want to see him. Her palms settled on her stomach and smoothed out her shirt. She kept her hands busy because if she didn't they would be rubbing her belly, looking for something that wasn't there yet. She hadn't begun to show yet and as long as she continued taking the pills Dommik gave her, her aches stayed away.

Dommik. Kat did want to see him but hated herself for admitting it. He hadn't approached her since they left Xan'Mara and she made no effort to find him.

She was just cold. Numb.

Or had been, until Earth was on the horizon and the thought of the open air filling her lungs made her excited. She caressed her stomach and sat back, blinking the screen from her eyes.

Will you be an Earth baby? She cooed to it in her mind. Her love for it growing by the second, already attached to her unborn child. It wasn't the parasite she was terrified of anymore. She had something in her now that she would die for, something beautiful and new, that she would go to the ends of the universe and back for.

She hated Dommik almost as much as she loved him. He had given her everything she wanted, needed, an adventure, a chance to grieve, and even a way to get over her paranoia. Kat glanced at the roach room. His methods were flawed, but they were *his* and he was *hers*.

It was enough. It felt like everything. And it burned as the cold thawed.

Kat found herself walking to the elevator, hoping her wristlet would work. It did.

It was hard to breathe as she rode to the upper decks in silence, as butterflies–*no*–Molucs filled her belly. The doors opened and she walked through the familiar passage past the alcove and its beautiful stars, past the medbay where the reader still sat on the table, further yet until the passageway opened up. She leaned to each new closed door to see if her wristlet would open them and wondered and wandered as nothing was barred off to her.

A maze of shadows and empty rooms lay around her and the cage she built around herself opened up a little bit more with each step forward.

Kat came across a lank of rope lying on the floor. It ended somewhere deep within the darkness beyond her sight. Her stomach flipped as she picked it up and tugged, finding no give in the cord.

She peered into the gloom as she pulled it again. Nothing.

"Dommik?" she called out.

Her face scrunched as she followed the rope's source, rolling it up over her arm as she went. It was smooth in her hands, well-used, with only the occasional knot she didn't stop to untie. The remaining doors forgotten.

The next light illuminated a lowered ceiling.

Not a lowered ceiling, she frowned, looking up at the crisscrossing pattern. *More rope.*

Kat reached up and pulled, but it remained stiff above her and retained its shape. *The same rope that's around my arm.*

"Dommik!?" she yelled.

She thought about turning back although she knew she wouldn't. Her need for answers bloomed within her and blurred out the rest. Safety wasn't an issue on the ship. Only her misgivings.

The pattern above her began to bleed out onto the walls on either side until it was so thick the walls were hidden. The dimness of the passageway petered close to black, the low-lights buried beneath. She gripped the ropes to find them, only to find her failure.

Kat jumped as a tendril fell and hit her shoulder. Her heart beat to the roar of a drum in her chest, filling her body with an uncontrollable need to shake it off, to shake everything off.

What the hell? What. The. Fuck? She resumed her pace with an adrenaline-fueled skip and continued forward. She wasn't afraid of the dark nor was she afraid of tight spaces, but as the thick threading enclosed around her, a rush of horror took the place of her curiosity. She found herself ducking and weaving through the ropes on all sides and as she went the smoothness of their length disappeared and was replaced by tears and frays.

The loose strands tickled against her like a thousand bugs crawling all over her body. And no matter how much she rubbed at her arms, her hair, her face, the feeling wouldn't go away.

A light appeared, casting a shadow against the clogging ropes, and the patterning askew. Kat rushed forward with her stomach in her throat.

Clawing, grasping, tugging, and panting until she reached the end.

Her eyes jumped around to stare at the room before her, the helm of the ship, the bridge, as her palms continued to brush off the invisible critters dancing on her skin.

A web. It's a web. Her eyes caught hold of something large moving above her.

Eight limbs, four arms and four legs, creeping from the corner to a thick length of long, silky black hair. Her back hit the bulky wall.

A face that looked like a skull, inhuman, with an extended metal jaw came next.

Sharp, dagger-like teeth flashed at her, dripping venom at the mouth only to pull taut at sun-bleached, phantom-like skin. It crept until it was directly overhead and the hair she knew so well fell in front of her.

"Dommik," Kat whispered to the-not-quite-a-spider, not-quite-a-man monstrosity staring down at her. "Come down," she gulped. "And talk to me." Her bladder had never felt so heavy.

The jaw shifted back into a beautifully tragic face.

"You're not afraid of me?" he snarled, his deep voice no more than a hiss between metal teeth.

Her gut flipped. "Should I be?" She squeezed her hands into fists, refusing to look away from him. "Is this...this is why I'm not allowed above? I understand now. I'm not afraid of you." Kat reached up and brushed her fingers through his hair to cup his head and pull him down to her. "Please come down."

She watched as Dommik's jaw shifted back into his head, soon followed by his legs that in turn landed like thunder before her, his extra arms went next until he was wholly humanoid again. Kat reached out to him but pulled her hands away, uncertain.

"That is my true form. My other half that powers a third of my mind, body, and machinery. I'm a spider. A Cyborg. A man. And each part of me, each piece of me wants to control. My DNA is not human and the child I seeded inside of you will not be entirely human as well."

Kat instinctively rounded her belly. "Will it be unwell?" The question tasted sour on her tongue. The thought of her baby being sickly scared her.

He crouched to his knees his arms rested over his thighs as he looped the cord around his palm. "No. It has nanocells running through its veins. Our baby will be perfect and if we're lucky will have your hair and your eyes."

Kat felt relieved and stifled at the same time. "I like your hair and eyes."

Dommik smirked up at her with a devilish twist. "Thank you."

She released her breath and stepped away from him to wander around the helm. The panoramic view of the universe was left alone as she eyed the console and the worn leather of the captain's chair. It was dark like the rest of the ship but brightened by the stars and the same silver aura. The webbing was all around her but unlike the rest of the passageway, there were piles of unused rope about and cigar butts lying in a tray. Kat could feel Dommik's eyes on her as she explored.

She turned full circle but was unable to find a second door. "How do your androids get to you?"

"They don't. They can't right now. The hallway is barred off and has been these past two weeks."

Kat turned to him. "Because of me?"

"Yes."

"I'm not sorry."

"I know. I was hoping you would come to me sooner. The wait has been miserable but now...now you've seen all of me." His hand waved around the room. "I have nothing left to hide."

She looked around the space again and up at the intricate webbing. At the dips and grooves between numerous metal brackets and the bizarre geometrical shapes throughout. It was beautiful and dreadful. But as she continued to stare at it, she found that she wasn't afraid of it or of him. It made her sad.

"Is this why you're alone?"

Dommik stood up and came to her. "No."

"Then why?"

"I hate the way people smell."

Kat looked down at herself. "What? Do I smell bad?"

He laughed as he pulled her horrified form into his arms. "Not you. You smell exotic, unusual, nice. I like it."

Ugh. "Thanks."

"You're welcome." He lifted her chin to look up at him. His eyes hollow and hopeful. "Will you stay with me? Here, on this ship, and we'll raise our child together. I'll take the webbing down, take only easy missions, take care of us."

Kat gnawed on her lip. "That's just it, Dommik. I came to tell you I quit."

Chapter Twenty-Three:

. . . . .

Kat watched as the hatch opened up to a dozen armed men and women. She had expected this, having seen it from the outside. She knew at this moment hundreds of people were watching the Monster Hunter unload his monsters and they'll be watching her too.

It was different when those guns were pointed in her direction.

Dommik stood beside her with his hand on her back. A man in a black suit approached them with Mia by his side. A triumphant look on her face.

"Dommik," the man nodded. "Katalina." He took her hand and shook it. "It's nice to finally meet you, although the circumstances could be better. My name is Mason."

His hand was sweaty in her palm. "Nice to meet you too, Mason." She wanted to wipe her hands over her pants but couldn't without being rude. She turned to Mia who graced her with an irritated glance, tablet in her face. Mia led her off the ship, bag in hand.

Dommik left her side as he turned to the off-boarding of the animals and plants; ground vehicles backed up to transport them to the port's quarantine facility.

Mia grumbled and waved her screen. "If I knew you were this easy to get rid of, I wouldn't have put so much effort in sending you to the Trentians." She turned and walked toward an aircraft, ushering her along. "We can finally put someone appropriate in the job. You have no idea how much more difficult you made things for me."

"It's nice to meet you too." Kat smiled and took shotgun, her bag on her lap. They drove through the landing zone and into a concrete tunnel. She twisted the key-chip between her fingers.

"There's nothing nice about this. Not only do I have to file all of your closing paperwork, I have to give you a fucking exit interview and for what? A month of mediocre work? Waste of my goddamned time."

Kat shrugged, "Make something up. I'll be out of your hair faster."

Mia humphed as the vehicle came to a stop. "Fine. Get out and go through that door," she pointed to a glass chamber where a series of guards stood by. "And fill these out." Mia handed her thumb drive. "When you're done hand it to Carl inside. Have a nice life, civilian."

Kat got out just in time for the craft to speed away. She entered the chamber and sat down as the computer scanned her body for pathogens and any other volatile things she may have picked up.

Dommik had run them down prior to his ship entering Earth's atmosphere. This second quarantine was to prevent the EPED from being liable for anything in between. Her foot tapped as the minutes passed.

"You're pregnant!" A man called out from the other side.

"I know," she yelled back.

233

"You get knocked up in space? Is that why you quit?"

Her foot tapped faster. "Yeah!"

"Sorry to hear that. You can come through now." The second door opened to a man on the other side, a set of earbuds dangled from his ears. The music was loud enough she could hear from across the room. New-age rap.

"Carl?" she asked.

"Yeah, that's me. I'll set you up over here."

Kat stretched her fingers and filled out the forms. She handed the drive over. "Done."

"Is it an alien's?"

"Is what an alien?"

"Your baby, is it a half-breed?"

She ignored him. "Where's the exit?"

"Fine. Fine, I have a big mouth. Go through that door and up the elevator to get to the port's entryway."

Kat had a job to do and only a short amount of time to do it. The second the elevator closed, her body twitched with excitement. The first thing she saw when it opened was the giant sign.

Welcome to space, it said. *Welcome to the gate to hell,* it meant. *Let's explore!*

Yes. Yes. Yes!

Her eyes left it to land on the tea stand where her feet jogged to. A middle-aged man stood behind the counter, his eyes glazed over with boredom as he wiped the same section of the counter over and over.

"Hi! John, right?" Kat couldn't contain her excitement. The man turned to her slowly while still wiping.

234

"Like it says on my name-tag. What tea would you like today?" His boredom was apparent.

Kat blushed, "Oh right, yes. Is your boss here? The woman with the scarves?"

He cocked his head and yelled making her flinch, "Marcy, you have a visitor!"

A series of noises sounded after, flustering words, and fallen boxes only to reveal a round woman draped in colors, patting off imaginary dust.

"Hello, dearie, what can I do for you? Well, you look familiar, are you one of Linda's girls? No, can't be, they're all blond. What has John done to upset you? I must say, he's a hard-worker but straight to the point. No upselling or razzle dazzle from him." Marcy shot him a look that could kill. "But a great worker nonetheless. How can I help you?"

Kat opened her mouth to speak–

"I remember you now! You're that girl. Two months ago, isn't it? Katie, Cassie, Kat! Kat, oh dear. Have you returned for the job?"

"No," she responded quickly.

"That's a shame. You see, my knees aren't what they used to be and John here, well, he doesn't sell much tea. Great man that he is."

Their faces opened up with surprise, startled and brilliant as they looked behind her. Heavy footsteps sounded. Her Cyborg's steps.

"We want to offer you a job, both of you," a hard, metalloid voice said. Kat's smile became a grin which became a happy laugh. Dommik stepped up next to her.

"Yes! Will you come work for us?"

Marcy's eyes went wide as she blatantly checked out the Cyborg twice over. Dommik straightened for her perusal.

"A job you say?"

"I need help on my ship. I could use two assistants and Kat here highly recommends you. You'll be paid handsomely." He reached down and took Marcy's hand, kissing the back of it.

John stepped forward. "You're that Cyborg, that Monster Hunter. We're not monster hunters. How can two tea merchants be of any use to you? What're you playing at?"

He was swatted away by scarves. "Oh dear, don't mind him! He meant no offense. Tell us about the job."

Kat looked around, noticing that they had a crowd, all staring at Dommik, all watching them. She took ahold of his hand and gripped it. *Mine.*

He's mine!

"I need help with the reporting, general maintenance, animal care, the works. You'll get to see the universe and many of its habitable and even inhabitable planets, free of charge, and the creatures that exist on them."

"What about aliens? Trentians. Will we get to see Trentians?" Marcy questioned.

"Possibly. Maybe."

Marcy looked ready to swoon with excitement. "In. I'm in. Let's do this. I want to find my alien suitor. Come on, John, let's pack our things."

Kat laughed as the woman began to close down the shop before her words left her.

"You don't have an alien suitor." Earning him a slap of a scarf. "But what about the tea stand? We can't just *leave*. We have shipments on the way, customers with orders, bills we have to pay."

"We'll buy it, everything, and it will be here when you come back. If you want to come back," Dommik interjected.

Kat placed her bag on the counter and handed it over, all of the money she had left from her grandmother. She couldn't stop laughing as Marcy and John blundered and packed, being hit over their heads with an adventure on the horizon.

"Mia's going to be so pissed." Her third-part spider, third-part Cyborg, and third-part man wrapped her up into his embrace. They shared a grin.

She turned into Dommik's arms and kissed him with everything she had to give.

Epilogue:

• • • •

Dommik sat back, unsure on how to move forward. The report sat like a dead weight on his screen, another obstacle, another possible stab at Kat's heart.

They had left Earth several days prior and were now heading to Ghost City, where he heard a rumor that Stryker was there and laying low. He still had his shipment loaded for him. Metal, Pryzian metal, enough to create one impenetrable mask.

He tried to hail him, tried to hail the other Monster Hunters, but so far he was only able to reach Netto, and Netto was not much of a talker.

Dommik looked at his security feed. It showed Marcy and John within his empty menagerie. His stress typically equated to how many beasts he had housed on his ship, but not this time.

He was going to be a father soon.

The news that sat before him would only bring up Kat's past and that was something he didn't want to do nor dwell on. Not when she was still recovering from the recent life changes he inflicted on her. Why shoot a dead horse? It's not like it would die again.

Dommik rubbed his thumb across his lips.

No secrets. They would keep nothing from each other. No matter how hard it was to share. No matter who it hurt.

He called Bin-One to his side. He and Kat took down the ropes that had bled out into the hallway, leaving them in coils in the captain's chamber, where he had begun to spin anew. Where they now both slept and designed the new space into a home befitting a Cyborg's family.

It still caught him off-guard. He had a family, a mate and a baby on the way and hopefully many more in the years to come. Little monsters of his own making, little insects of his own. He hoped for a daughter. An Arachne to fill his heart.

Dommik felt himself evolve into something more than just a bestial machine.

"Tell Kat to meet me in the bridge," he mumbled as he watched the stars fly by.

"Yes, Master."

It wasn't long before her scent reached his nose, breezing through the small corridor. He was addicted to it and still wanted to bottle it up for his own personal use. Her footsteps sounded next, light and quick, heading toward him without fear. It was her voice that had him swiveling around.

"Hey," she breathed and smiled. "You called?" Her eyes laughed at him, wild and bright and filled with so much life, enough to feed the both of them.

Dommik grabbed her wildness and settled it in his lap. "I did." He buried his nose in her hair. "I missed you, but I also have something to show you."

Kat turned in his lap and straddled him. "Oh? Is it something frightening? I'm beginning to like you scary." She moved against him and he got caught up in her cute seduction.

"Is that so?"

"Yeah, that's so." She brushed her fingers through his hair, releasing it from its band to twirl and tug it. He closed his eyes.

"I'll have to find more reasons to be scary, since you've already seen the worst parts of me."

"The best parts of you." He felt the brush of her lips settle over his to place a silky kiss. Soft and sweet and everything he wasn't.

"I love you," he whispered between them.

"I love to hate you. Unfortunately, I just love you too."

"Good enough for me." Dommik pulled her tight against him and relished the moment. That one moment when bliss was within your grasp and life, for all its rough edges, was good.

He spun his chair back toward the screen and let the moment slip away. The file was open for her viewing.

"This is what I want to show you. I received it today from Dr. Cagley. Apparently, she looked into your case files and found something about your grandmother that I don't think you knew." Kat tensed and turned her face toward the console. "You don't have to read it if you don't want to," he hedged, hoping.

She was absorbed before he even stopped speaking. He held onto her as she read about her grandmother's medical history, all of it out there for her to take in and whether she found it good or bad, he was going to be there.

Minutes passed by and Kat remained quiet on his lap, staring at the screen, and he smelled the trickle of her tears before they shed from her eyes.

"So. I'm crazy. Plain psychotic," she wilted and looked away, then laughed high and loud. "I don't care. I just. Don't. Care."

"I didn't want to keep this from you..."

"She was immune. Immune! I didn't know that and I thought...when she died. She couldn't have had what my parents had."

"They gave it to her to save you, Kat. They tested and treated her while you were locked up. They had you both locked up. Her immunity saved your life." Dommik pulled her back into his embrace. Kat didn't fight him. "You're not crazy."

She shook her head. "Why did she keep it from me?"

I wish I knew. I wish I knew everything for you. "Because she loved you."

They sat there in the dim light of the bridge as the stars twinkled and the seconds turned into minutes. He held her as her tears dried on her eyelashes and her body softened against his. Dommik gave her his warmth as she drifted in and out of sleep. Even as messages pinged through the system and new missives went ignored. There was nothing but the two of them.

Kat awoke sometime later, turning her glassy green eyes up to his. "Thank you," she said.

"For what?"

"For...well, for everything. For taking me up into the stars with you." Her hands went around his neck. "For showing me what's beyond my walls." Her smile returned. "I really do love you too."

"Oh, good. I was worried." Dommik smiled. "To the future?"

241

She nodded. "To the future." Her wildness bloomed. Her wings restored.

"Well, then, let's catch us some monsters!"

Author's Note:

· · · ·

T hank you for reading Wild Blood, the spider and the cat, first in the Cyborg Shifter's series. If you liked the story or had a comment please leave me a review!

If you love cyborgs, aliens, anti-heroes, and adventure, follow me on facebook or through my blog online for information on new releases and updates.

Join my "work in progress" newsletter for the same information.

Turn the page for the blurb for Storm Surge, Cyborg Shifters Book Two.

Naomi Lucas

Storm Surge

· · · ·

Everybody feared the man with the metal band over his mouth.

Stryker was part of an elite group of Cyborgs genetically enhanced with inhuman DNA. He was known as the Creeper, the quiet, the man with half a face. His fate was his own and his freedom hard-earned, having nothing to live for but the hunt and his perfect record. Until he encountered a distress call that changed his bleak existence. A distress call he couldn't ignore.

"Please, oh God, please. Is anybody out there? This is Norah Lee, a scientist of Earth. I–I don't know what to do. I think everybody...everyone is dead. Please if you hear this, please help us.

I can hear them outside. They're coming...

I don't want to die!"

About the Author

Naomi Lucas is an indie author who is struggling to navigate the intricacies of social media. She loves being creative whether its with painting, writing, or making little jingles about her dog, Barracuda, or her cat,   Daliah,   in   the   car.

But more importantly, she is a coffee addict with a lustful, burning desire to visit the Starbucks Factory in Seattle and never leave.

Read more at <u>Naomi Lucas's site</u>.

88100146R00146

Made in the USA
Middletown, DE
06 September 2018